# SALACIOUS EXPOSURE

## SEATTLE DOMS

BECCA JAMESON

# CHAPTER 1

## FAYE

"I can't believe you talked me into this," I hiss as I lean toward my friend and co-worker, grabbing her arm. "This is so not my scene."

Trinity turns in her seat and smiles at me. "It's just an intro class, Faye. You don't have to commit to a membership or anything."

"You say that like it's intro to algebra or intro to poly sci," I whisper.

Trinity giggles, covering her mouth to stifle the noise as everyone takes their seats. She shrugs. "Intro to algebra. Intro to BDSM. It's all the same."

I glance around the room and shudder. I don't know a thing about BDSM. I should have done some research before I let Trinity talk me into this. I should have stayed home and read the latest issue of *Science Weekly*. That's the kind of information I should be filling my brain with—not BDSM.

A man at the front claps his hands together. "I want to thank all of you for coming tonight. My name is Easton. I'm one of the owners of Edge. Whether you're new to BDSM, new to Seattle, or just curious, welcome. I'll be giving you a crash course in what BDSM is all about, then I'll take some questions, and finally, you're all free to wander around and explore the club before it opens to our regular members."

Easton... I knew an Easton once. Easton Riley. He didn't look anything like this tall, buff, energetic, friendly man. The only thing this sexy Easton has in common with the Easton I knew in high school is his hair color.

I find myself mesmerized by this man. For one thing, he's charismatic. I assume everyone in the room is mesmerized by him. For another thing, he surprises me. For some reason, I expected the owner of a fetish club to be...well, not so...regular.

Easton is an ordinary man. Mid-thirties, brown hair, brown eyes, tanned skin. If he has any tattoos, I can't see them. He's wearing a black polo shirt that fits snugly around his enormous biceps. He has on blue jeans and tennis shoes.

Why did I expect leather and chains? I had visions of bikers. I'm so shallow.

I try to listen to what he's telling us about the meaning of the BDSM acronym and the general rules of the club and the fetish community in general. It's hard to focus, though, because I keep finding myself simply staring at him—the way he moves as he paces slowly back and forth. He's so confident. Every time he turns to one side, I catch a glimpse of his fantastic ass in those worn jeans. His thighs are rock-hard. The outline of his chest and abs under the tight shirt is magazine-worthy—and certainly not featured in the science magazines I usually read.

He moves on from his basic introduction to talking about various items used for impact play. I hold my breath through a lot of this, shocked by how ordinary he acts about each item as he holds it up—paddles, floggers, crops, whips, and something called a cat o' nine tails that looks like it could do some serious damage.

I wince and jerk in my seat when he flicks his wrist, making the evil torture device strike the table behind him.

I've avoided looking around the room too much because it's overwhelming. We're sitting in the middle of what he calls a playroom. It's huge. The floor, walls, and ceiling are all a deep purple. He explains that the lighting is significantly dimmer when the club is open. For this class, they have turned on all the recessed lighting.

I feel lightheaded as he tells us about all the apparatuses in the room: spanking benches, St. Andrew's crosses, cages, a spider web, and sex swings. I sit on my hands to keep them from trembling as he points out an area for medical play, another for fire play, and another for blood play. He glosses over a lot of the sections, leaving me wondering. Blood play? What the heck?

Three sides of the room have half walls that separate the various play areas without obstructing anyone's ability to view the scenes. One side of the room has a stage for performances and auction nights.

He points to a hallway in one corner and informs us there are private rooms that can be reserved. Themed rooms. I don't even want to know what those themes might be. I shudder. Some of the rooms are apparently for aftercare. Everything is included in the monthly membership fee as long as they are available. Apparently, members can reserve sections.

"It's so exciting," Trinity whispers in my ear as Easton finishes his Intro to BDSM 101 class.

I'm not sure exciting is the word I would use, but I'm oddly intrigued, which is unnerving.

Easton stops pacing to face us. "A few of our members will be around the room to demonstrate the apparatuses. Feel free to wander. Ask questions. If you're interested in a membership, you can speak to me or my brother. He got caught on a call in the office upstairs, but he'll be down shortly."

As people stand and slowly make their way around the room, exploring, Trinity jumps up. "It looks like someone is going to demonstrate that cross." She points to one of the sections of the room. "I'm going to go watch. You coming?"

"Yep. Sure. I'll follow you."

She spins around and takes off. I'm not actually quite ready to stand yet, and I'm also not sure my legs will hold me up.

When I finally push to stand up, I notice a few people gathering at a spanking bench. That seems less intimidating than the St. Andrew's cross, so I shuffle closer to watch.

A man dressed in all black helps a woman in a short black dress climb onto the bench. He guides her elbows and knees to padded sections, arranging her as she gets comfortable.

I suck in a breath when he secures her ankles and wrists, drawn closer to the unfolding scene. The man takes his time, circling her, running his hands over her body. He lowers his face to her ear and whispers something I can't hear.

The woman shudders.

When he rounds behind her and flattens his palms on her thighs, I flinch. I can't help but cross my arms, and then I slide one hand up to my mouth as I squeeze my legs together.

I'm wearing black slacks, a cream sweater, and black flats. It seemed like a good choice while I was still at home. Now, I see it wouldn't have mattered what I wore. Most of the people who've come to attend this introductory class are wearing casual clothes. After all, we'll be gone before the club actually opens.

The man slides his hands up her thighs, pushing her skirt higher and higher until he flips it up onto her back, leaving her butt cheeks exposed. All she's wearing under the skirt is a black G-string.

I've never understood G-strings. They look so uncomfortable. Why would anyone want that elastic up between their butt cheeks all day?

Maybe I'm a prude. Okay, I'm definitely a prude. There's no *maybe* about it. I wear sensible, plain white underwear. White bras, too. I don't have time or the inclination to shop for something prettier. Something sexier. Who would see them anyway?

The man comes to one side of the woman, molds his palm to her butt for long seconds, and then lifts his hand and gives her a firm swat.

I gasp as my entire body flinches. The woman's skin pinkens, showing exactly where he spanked her. I have no idea why I'm affected by this. Why would anyone want to be strapped down and beaten?

My mouth is dry, and I can't seem to bring myself to

lick my lips. I'm practically hugging myself. My nipples are hard, and there's a weird flutter in my stomach.

"Faye?"

I jerk my gaze to my left at the sound of my name coming from the club owner. I know it's him before I look because I've memorized his mesmerizing tone of voice. Why does he know my name? "Uh..."

"It *is* you. Faye Lunsford," he whispers. "You probably don't remember me. We went to the same high school. You were a freshman when I was a senior. We were in debate club together."

*Ohmygod.* This is the same Easton I knew in high school. I stare at him with wide eyes, probably looking like a deer in the headlights. How the hell does he remember me?

I was a quiet, meek, awkward girl my freshman year. My parents insisted I join the debate club to help me learn to speak to other people. I don't think it helped. Fifteen years later, I'm still quiet, meek, and awkward.

Easton sets a hand on my elbow and gently guides me away from the scene. He grins. "You don't remember me, do you?" He smiles.

I swallow. "Yes. I mean, I remember there was an Easton Riley in my debate club. But you're...uh...buff." Buff? Lordy, what's wrong with me?

He chuckles. "Yeah, I grew about six inches after high school and started working out. I could say the same about you." He lifts a brow, his mouth still turned up in a devastatingly sexy smile.

"I'm buff?"

He laughs again. "No. Not buff. How about...curvy? Is that inappropriate?"

6

I bite my bottom lip, staring at him. He's not wrong. At fifteen, I was still flat-chested and gangly. I've changed.

"I guess you live in Seattle, then?" he asks.

I nod. "I moved back here a few months ago." I look around and state the obvious. "You own a club."

"With my brother, Drake, yes. We opened Edge seven years ago."

I don't have a single clue what to say. Easton exudes confidence. He hasn't taken his gaze off mine. I guess debate club served him well if his goal was to excel at speaking to people.

"Are you interested in a membership?"

"Oh, no. I just came with my friend, Trinity. She dragged me out tonight. BSDM isn't really my thing."

He chuckles. "*BDSM*. Don't worry; you're not the first person to swap the acronym. It's common."

My face heats. I should keep my mouth closed. In fact, I purse my lips.

He nods toward the spanking scene I'd been watching. "It looked like you were engrossed. Maybe you should give it a try."

I jerk my gaze from where the woman is being thoroughly spanked now, trying not to react to her reddened skin or the moans coming from her mouth. When I look back at Easton, I shake my head. "I don't think so. I'm not really any more outgoing than I was in high school."

"Are you sure? Can't hurt to come a few nights and watch. I'd be happy to sponsor your membership so you can try it out."

I flinch. "I can afford my own membership," I retort a bit too harshly. I have no idea what the membership fees even are. I should think before I speak. Nevertheless, I make good money. I'm smart with it, too. I save fifty percent of my salary for retirement. A part of me wants to tell Easton this so he doesn't think I'm a charity case. Instead, I purse my lips again.

"I didn't mean to insult you, Faye," he says gently. "It's not uncommon for someone to sponsor a new member so they can try out the club, especially this second floor."

"Are there different membership tiers?"

He nods. "Yes. You probably saw the first floor before you came upstairs. The fees for that floor are a hundred dollars a year. Membership to the first floor covers our high-end dance club. This second floor is five hundred dollars a month."

My eyes widened. Five hundred dollars a month? Wow.

"It's a commitment. Every member is well-vetted. Most members come at least once a month, some every weekend, or even more than once a week. We offer a safe place to engage in many lifestyle preferences."

He's standing so close to me, keeping his voice down so as not to disturb any of the demonstrations. His scent is as intoxicating as his voice. I find myself oddly attracted to him, which is not like me.

I'm never attracted to anyone. I'm a focused career woman. I have a PhD in biology. I have no interest in dallying with men. I've been a wallflower all my life, and I've come to terms with it.

With every passing year, I become more certain that I should remain single. At thirty-one, I've already watched several acquaintances get divorced, some more than once. The mating game seems ridiculous, and I'm not interested in playing.

My single co-workers go through a repetitive ritual

that makes me wonder if they're playing with a full deck. They go out on Friday nights, drink too much, hook up with men, spend a few weeks oohing and ahhing excitedly as if the man were a god, and then realize he's not as great as they thought, break up, and start it all over again.

It's the oddest ritual. Why bother? I'm perfectly happy being alone. I have everything I need. My apartment is exactly how I want it. When I come home at night, everything is where I left it in the morning. I know what's in my fridge. I don't have to clean up after anyone but myself. I'm well aware I have odd tendencies, but I don't care, and I'm not bothering anyone.

Relationships are overrated. I don't need one.

The truth is I was the weird girl in high school. People made fun of me. They laughed at my expense. Maybe I'm not as weird now as I was then because I'm no longer gangly with a mouth full of braces, but being bullied leaves a mark on a person that never fully goes away.

Even after I filled out and learned how to take care of my hair and put on makeup, I never lost that feeling that people are whispering about me behind my back.

Easton reaches into his back pocket and pulls out a card. He holds it out to me. "Think about it. My number's on the back. Call me if you decide you want to come back. No obligation necessary. You could just spend some time watching. Many new members do nothing but watch for months. For some people, watching is exactly what they enjoy. For others, they find themselves drawn to certain aspects of the lifestyle and decide to try them out."

I stare at the card. He isn't trembling like I am. This man is confident and strong. He's probably also Dominant. After all, he owns the club.

Finally, I take the card from him. To be polite.

9

"Thank you." I'll never call him. I couldn't, but he doesn't need to know that.

He smiles warmly. "I hope you call, Faye. I think you'd enjoy Edge." As he turns and walks away, I stare at his retreating form. He's mouthwatering.

What the hell is wrong with me? I don't ever find people to be mouthwatering. That's a stupid word and a stupid reaction.

I jerk myself out of my ridiculous thoughts and look around for Trinity. Luckily, it's almost time to leave. The club opens soon. Anyone who hasn't secured a membership has to leave before it opens.

Thank God.

# CHAPTER 2

EASTON

"Who was that woman you were talking to earlier?" Drake asks me several hours later.

We're in our office on the third floor, monitoring all three levels of our club. "What woman?" I know who he's talking about, but I don't want to give him the impression I care. I *don't* care. Faye can do whatever she wants. I approached her for the same reason I approach anyone after an intro class. She looked intrigued. She should come try out the club. I offer that same thing to lots of people.

Drake smirks. "Don't try that shit with me, Easton. You know who I'm talking about. Sexy strawberry blond, who looked like she'd never heard of a fetish club, let alone seen the inside of one," he teases.

It was that strawberry-blond hair that caught my attention and reminded me of the girl I'd known in high school. I noticed her even before I began the class. It was a struggle to ignore her while I spoke. When I approached her afterward, I grew confident it was indeed Faye.

Other than her hair, the woman has very little resemblance to her high school self. Granted, I only knew her when she was a freshman. It's possible she filled out and matured before she was even eighteen, but I was in college then.

"Ah," I say, pretending to just now remember, "that was Faye Lunsford. We went to high school with her."

"Faye Lunsford... I don't remember her."

"You probably wouldn't. She was a freshman when we were seniors. She was in the debate club. You weren't."

"Ah." Drake smirks. "Did she look like that back then?"

"Nope. I only recognized the hair." I glance down at my own body. "We didn't look like this either. Not even at eighteen, if you recall."

Drake chuckles. "Like I could forget. Could we have been any dorkier?"

"Nope, but we outgrew it. The joke is on anyone who bullied us back then. I laugh every time I'm at the bank."

Drake nods. "Ain't that the truth? Did you offer her a sponsorship?"

"I tried. I doubt she'll take me up on it, though. She was way out of her element."

"Did you get her number?"

"Fuck no," I retort.

"Why the hell not? She's hot. You were obviously engrossed in her."

I narrow my gaze at Drake. "The sheets aren't even cooled down on my bed from the inferno that broke up with me last week, dude. I'm not interested in a repeat."

Drake rolls his eyes. "Bethany was a bitch."

I glare at him. "Bethany was my girlfriend for six months. Did you think she was a bitch the entire time?"

"No, but I realized she wasn't right for you before you did."

"Just because she wanted more out of our relationship than I was willing to give her doesn't make her a bitch. It just makes us incompatible." Why am I defending the woman?

"Do not start doubting your abilities as a Dominant, Easton. You're one of the best Doms I know."

"But not *quite* good enough for Bethany," I respond with snark.

Drake shakes his head. "Don't go there. Besides the fact that Bethany turned out to be pretentious, she wanted you to hurt her. *Injure* her. Neither of us enjoys that sort of thing, and we only permit it in Edge after careful consideration. Injuring a sub is not our thing. You know that."

"There are submissives who enjoy a deeper pain." Again, why am I defending Bethany? Because she made me feel inadequate, and that pisses me off.

Drake narrows his gaze at me. "Easton, stop it. Nothing you did was good enough for her. She wanted more pain, and you gave it to her. She wanted bruising, and I know you hated striking her that hard. I couldn't have done it. Then, she wanted blood. She was thirsty for it. If you had struck her until her skin split, she would've been satisfied with that level of dominance for about a month before she demanded what? A broken bone? She needs help, Easton. Not a Dominant."

I blow out a breath. "You're right."

"So...Faye. You know her name. Hunt her down. I bet you could find her easily."

"Assuming Lunsford is still her last name. She could be married or divorced." She didn't correct me when I supplied her name, though, so I'm betting she's not married.

Drake spins around in his chair and jiggles his mouse. Before I can stop him, Faye's face is on the computer screen. "Wow... I'm impressed. Look at that. Didn't even have to go to social media. Faye Lunsford is an accomplished woman who only needs a Google search."

Against my better judgment, I drop into the chair next to Drake and look over his shoulder. *Damn.*

"Did she tell you she's an accomplished biologist with a PhD?"

I rub my face. "No. I didn't ask. She only told me she recently moved back to Seattle."

"Yep. She sure did. Because she got this dream job with one of the best pharmaceutical companies in the world. She's published. Look at all the articles she's written..."

I'm impressed. I shouldn't be. I knew she was a bright student even in high school. She might have hated public speaking, but when she spoke, brilliance came out of her mouth. I'm not shocked she has a PhD in biology.

Drake grabs a sticky note and scribbles on it before handing it to me. Her phone number, email address, and physical address. "Tuck that in your pocket. Give it a few days. Call her."

I snatch it from his hand and stuff it in my pocket, but I'm not calling Faye Lunsford. She's a temptation I don't need. I'm not jumping into something with another woman. Like I told Drake, my bed is still overheated from

Bethany. It's going to take a long time for the sheets to cool down. It's going to take a longer time for me to be willing to put my heart out there and trust again. I don't need a woman in my life. I'm perfectly happy without the stress.

But damn, Faye tugged at me. She's nothing like any woman I've ever dated. She may be inherently submissive, but she has no training. When and if I put myself out there again, I sure don't want to guide anyone through the steps of learning what their preferred kink is. It's tedious. It takes a lot of energy and time.

I rise and leave the room, mumbling something about checking on how things are going on the first floor. We have people monitoring every floor. They don't need me. I just need an excuse to get away from my brother. He knows me too well. I can't think around him.

As soon as I descend from our third-floor office to our first-floor office, I step into the room, shut the door, and plop down on my chair. I run my hands through my hair and stare at the ceiling.

I can't get Faye out of my head. She's a bombshell. Gone is the skinny girl who started high school with a flat chest and stick legs. Faye has curves now. Amazing fucking hot curves. Surely, she has a boyfriend. He's probably vanilla.

Or maybe she doesn't. After all, she's only been in Seattle a few months. She probably wouldn't have visited a BDSM club if she were attached to someone.

Again, why do I care? If she calls, which isn't likely, I'll set her up with a temporary membership and introduce her to a few Doms I trust with newbies. She can try some things out. Or she can just watch. I won't interfere.

Who am I kidding? If Faye decides to come to Edge, I

will sit right here in my office and watch her sexy body on the monitor every moment she's in the building. I'll be jealous doing it, too.

Even though I don't train subs because it's too tedious, I find myself itching to train Faye. I want to show her every damn thing and watch her reactions. I'm salivating over the idea of seeing her cheeks pinken, watching her fidget, and staring at her thighs when she squeezes them together.

Chances are in the end, someone like Faye will end up finding BDSM to be way too much for her. She might be able to come in a few weekends and watch, but she also might be horrified and not return after an hour. She's so green and so vanilla.

Doesn't matter. She won't call.

# CHAPTER 3

FAYE

Why do I still have Easton's card, and why is it sitting propped up against my computer monitor?

Every evening when I get home from work and sit down at my home computer, I'm faced with that card. It taunts me. It's like a siren, whispering at me. *You know you want to. You know you're curious.*

It's been two weeks since I went to that BDSM class. Since then, I've spent about an hour every evening researching BDSM. I'm a researcher after all. Research is what I live for. I don't even go to a new restaurant without checking their ratings, reviews, and menu selections first.

When I went to the zoo last weekend—to keep my mind off of Easton—I spent three days prior researching everything the Seattle zoo had to offer, plotting out my day, and even deciding where I would eat lunch and which items I would order from the menu.

I finger the card, pick it up, look at it, then flip it over.

I've memorized his number. I don't need the card. I'll know his number twenty years from now. My memory isn't exactly eidetic but close. When I want to know something, I won't forget it.

I prop the card back against my computer, check the time, and click on the open tab for the site I was researching yesterday. I only allow myself an hour a night. I could get sucked into something and look up and find the sun coming up if I'm not careful.

I set my alarm and start reading. I've read a lot. This isn't new information. I keep glancing at the card. Eventually, I lean back in my chair and close my eyes. Two things keep going through my mind. One of them is Easton. Thoughts of him consume me, especially when I'm trying to go to sleep. I've lost sleep for the past two weeks.

The other thing that infiltrates my mind is the visual of that woman on the spanking bench. I breathe heavier every time I think of her strapped to that padded bench, her ass on display all pink and hot. The way she moaned... I nearly moaned with her. I nearly moan every time I think about it.

And I'm fixated. I've tried reading my favorite science journals. I've tried watching documentaries. I've tried listening to music. Nothing blocks out the visuals in my head.

Maybe I should take Easton's offer and go to the club. He said I could just visit and observe. I don't have to participate in anything. I could just watch and get this fixation out of my system.

But what about my obsession with Easton himself? The man is way out of my league. I looked him up. He and his brother developed an app before they even graduated from college. Apparently, they sold it for a lot of money and went on to research and develop more apps.

I need to shake him from my system. Seeing him in person is not going to help. I have ridiculous, irrational thoughts about him that are pure fiction.

I've used my vibrator so many times in the past two weeks it's probably going to stop charging. I bet I've masturbated more since I went to Edge than all the times in the past year combined.

I'm usually focused on nothing but work. When I get home at night, I have a routine. It doesn't include men. I don't have any interest in dating or letting anyone into my life. I'm a solitary person. Relationships aren't my gig.

Before I went to Edge, I masturbated to thoughts of fake men without faces who slid between the sheets with me in a hotel—not my home. They stroked my clit until I came. That's it. They didn't penetrate me. I didn't touch them. I just needed to pretend human fingers touched me while I held my favorite vibrator against my clit.

Now, it's like a whole new world has opened up to me. I'm not sure it's a good thing. For one thing, I visualize much kinkier activities. I'm at the club. I'm restrained. I'm exposed. People are watching me, and I can't stop the fact that I come in front of them. I don't even need contact with my clit. I come from being exposed.

Surely, my thoughts aren't normal. Though how would I ever know? I certainly wouldn't tell a living soul what's been going through my head. Not even Trinity.

The man who dominates me is not headless. He's always Easton. Every night, my thoughts have expanded. He's started touching me. He reaches between my legs and strokes my folds.

I can orgasm in under two minutes. I've never been able to do that before. I also think about it during the day. I can't wait to get home, take my shower, get in bed, and grab my vibrator. It's like a drug. I need my daily fix of imaginary Easton commanding me.

I should just call him, accept his generous offer, and visit the club. Maybe I can flush it out of my system with one visit. Maybe two. It won't kill me to go four times, once a week for a month.

Easton must be a busy man when the club is open. He and his brother own it. I probably won't even see either of them. I'll just be a voyeur, standing in the shadows, watching.

I glance at his card again. I can't believe I'm considering this idea. It's been two weeks, though, and I've developed an unhealthy relationship with what I imagine happens at Edge. I bet I'm exaggerating what the experience would be like. I bet if I went, I would find out what I felt while watching that scene was an anomaly.

The next time I go, nothing will affect me like that did. It was a fluke. I should get it out of my system so I can put it behind me and continue with my regularly scheduled life. The one that doesn't include sex clubs and buff men.

I pick up my phone with shaky fingers and stare at it. I don't have to call him. I could just text. It's seven o'clock. The club doesn't open until eight. Easton might be busy, though. I won't be offended if he doesn't respond tonight. It might take him a day or two to get back to me.

It's actually a good plan. I'll text him now. He'll be busy. It will give me time to think about my crazy plan before he responds.

I type in his number. I consider adding it to my

contacts, but decide against it. I don't need Easton in my phone. This communication is only to establish my temporary membership. We won't be corresponding after this one time. Taking a deep breath, I compose a text and stare at it for a minute, making sure I spelled everything correctly and building up the guts to hit send.

> Hi. This is Faye Lunsford. I've been thinking about your offer to visit the club. If your offer still stands, I'd like to take you up on it. My curiosity is piqued. I would just want to observe. I'm not interested in more. Maybe one day next month would be convenient? Thank you for your consideration.

Does it sound too formal? Too stilted? I'm not good at social cues. Or social anything, really. I was a wallflower in high school, and I'm still a wallflower. I like it. I like to watch people. I find them fascinating. And nothing has ever been more fascinating than observing the members of Edge.

I finally hit send and then blow out a breath. It's done. I won't think about it again. If he responds in a few days, great. If not, then I need to let this weird obsession go.

I nearly jump out of my seat when my phone suddenly rings in my hand. I stare at it in shock. The incoming call is from Easton's number. Why is he calling? He could have just responded to my text. I nearly drop the phone before I manage to answer it. "Hello?" My voice is faint.

"Hey, Faye. I'm so glad you texted. I was beginning to think you wouldn't. It's been two weeks."

"Well, I, uh, needed to do some research and, uh..." I

sound like a fool. I cringe and bite my lip to stop myself from speaking.

"Research is good. I'm glad you did that. You'll be less shocked by what you see in the club if you've done some reading on the subject."

I lick my lips, surprised by his casual reaction. Thankfully, my words weren't as dorky as they sounded coming out of my mouth.

"Why don't you come in tonight?"

My breath hitches. *Tonight?* Is he serious? "Uh, I wasn't planning to go out tonight. I figured next month sometime. I thought you would need more notice. Don't I need to fill out forms and get a background check and stuff?"

He chuckles. "You do need to fill out some forms. You can do them from home if you'd like. I assume you're not a serial killer or an abusive Dominant who's been kicked out of several other clubs for violating the rules."

I flinch. "Uh, no. I'm not either of those things."

"Text me your email. I'll send you the forms. You can return them through email and come over. We open at eight. I can show you around or get someone else to do so if you'd rather. Or you're also welcome to explore on your own."

"It won't bother anyone for me to observe them?"

"Goodness no. A lot of people enjoy being watched. Many of the people who do public scenes do so because it's titillating knowing people are watching them."

Tonight, though? I wasn't planning on going there tonight or even next week. I need to work up the nerve first. I was thinking along the lines of three weeks from now. I could put it on my calendar. Plan for it. Emotionally.

I glance at the paper planner I have on my desk and wince. I don't have anything planned for tonight. My neat handwriting indicates I plan to jog tomorrow morning on my treadmill at eight. I intend to start my laundry at ten and go to the grocery store while the washer runs. I'm pathetic.

"Don't overthink it, Faye," he says gently. "Just come in. No obligation. Like you said, satisfy your curiosity."

I don't have any excuses. Maybe I should be spontaneous and just go. Then, I won't spend three weeks fretting over it. "Um, okay. I guess I could do that. What should I wear?"

"We do have a dress code. No T-shirts, no logos, no jeans, no tennis shoes. Slacks or a dress are preferred. A blouse and skirt. Whatever you're comfortable in. You can wear flats or heels."

I wince. "I don't do well in heels."

"Then wear flats. There will be people here in all kinds of fetish wear. Some will be in extremely revealing lingerie. Some will be naked."

I draw in a breath. I can't believe I'm considering this —a club where people will be naked. I've never seen a naked adult. I don't even watch porn. I considered it a few times this week for the first time in my life and then nixed the idea for fear that I would end up with a virus on my computer.

"Okay," I whisper.

"You can get here whenever you want, Faye. I'll leave your name with Jax at the entrance downstairs. He'll let you in and arrange for someone to escort you to the stairs so you can get to the second floor. Marny will be working the reception desk on the second floor tonight. I'll tell her to expect you."

It's so complicated. I'm not sure I fully absorbed everything he just said. I usually pay such close attention to directions. I'm so out of my element that I fear I missed something.

"I'll text all of that to you, Faye," he adds in a kind voice. Maybe he read my mind. I'm okay with that.

"Thank you."

"See you soon."

I'm shaking as he ends the call. Afraid I might drop the phone, I set it on the desk and take a deep breath. I'm going to Edge tonight. I've taken leave of my senses.

# CHAPTER 4

## EASTON

"You made it." I'm actually surprised she has shown up. She was so timid both when I saw her and on the phone earlier. I know coming to Edge is a stretch for her.

I lean in and air kiss her cheek, inhaling her scent. Vanilla and Faye.

She's stunning. Her strawberry-blond hair hangs halfway down her back, the front pulled up in a clip. She has on very little makeup—mascara and lip gloss, I think.

She's wearing a black dress. It's demure, and I suspect she only owns demure clothes. She can't hide her fantastic tits, though. The spandex material gives me an eyeful even though they're fully covered.

The dress reaches almost to her knees, and the skirt is loose and flowy. She has on black ballet slippers, pearl earrings, a pearl necklace, and a matching bracelet. She could be going on a date, to the theater, or to her grandmother's house for dinner.

Or to my BDSM club.

"Am I dressed okay?" she asks in a soft voice.

"Perfect, Faye. Like I said, anything goes here, really." I set my palm on her elbow and guide her away from the reception area and into the club.

Her breath hitches. "Oh, it's a lot different without all the lights on."

I pause just inside the entrance and look around. "Yes. It's all about ambiance. What do you think?"

"I love the deep purple. It's rich and elegant."

"I'm glad you like it." I fight the urge to chuckle. About a dozen scenes are going on in this room. It's almost ten o'clock. The club is in full swing, and Faye chooses to comment on the lighting.

I glance down and note she has nothing with her. "I assume Marny showed you where the lockers are?"

"Yes. I put my coat and purse in one."

"Good. Phones are not permitted on this floor. For one thing, absolutely no photography is allowed, but we also don't want someone's phone to suddenly ring and disrupt a scene."

She nods. She's rubbing her palms together in front of her. She's very nervous.

I'm torn. I've thought about this woman far more often than I should have for the past two weeks. What is my obsession? Sure, she's stunning. Heads are going to turn. But it's something else.

It's her innocence. She's so green. I get the feeling it's not just BDSM. I feel like she's pretty innocent in general. I want to know how many men she's slept with and if they took care of her. Something about her makes me think that number is low.

I don't play with newbies. I don't have the patience

for it. I don't train subs. I don't even give them a tour. And yet, I find myself wanting all of that with Faye. I need to back the fuck off and get a grip.

I'm not the man for Faye. I'm not even the man for anyone right now. I'm jaded. Before Bethany, I considered myself a strong Dom. She shook my foundation a bit. Even though intellectually, I know she was the one in the wrong, she made me feel inadequate.

I've never been with anyone who felt like they weren't getting enough from me as a Dominant. It's historically always been the opposite. I can be overbearing, controlling, and demanding.

When I scene with women inside the club, they end our session wrung out. I waste no time bringing them to a deep submission. When I'm in a relationship that extends outside of the club, I'm still very commanding. I've never moved a woman into my home, partly because I'm aware I have trouble turning off my Dom. Or maybe it has more to do with the fact that I've never met a woman I wanted to spend that much time with.

Even Bethany didn't live with me. She spent the night on weekends, sometimes, but she never had a drawer or even a toothbrush. Every time I considered taking that step and suggesting she leave some things at my place, something held me back. I suspect I knew months ago that we weren't quite right together.

Bethany was the first woman I've ever dated who could submit as deeply as I crave, and then she took things too far. It wasn't that she wanted to submit to me more hours of the day; it was that she wanted to submit on a level that crossed the line.

I shake my ex from my head. She doesn't deserve to

take up so much space—nor should I let her hold any power over me. It's ironic how much power I let her maintain. She's gone. I'm not even sorry or sad. I'm simply shaken. My foundation was tested.

I look at Faye and find her looking around the main floor with wide eyes. Her breaths are shallow. Again, I remind myself she's the polar opposite of what I look for in a sub.

Oh, she's submissive. There's no doubt. But fuck. Does she know it? Normally, I would pass someone like her off to another Dom to show her the ropes. However, the thought of passing Faye off doesn't sit well with me. I want to train her myself. I want to own her firsts. I want to watch her blossom.

"You don't have to babysit me," she says. "I'm a big girl. I can wander around and watch. I bet you have better things to do."

"I don't mind showing you around for a while." I try to make my tone indifferent, but I'm not sure I succeed. I nod toward a St. Andrew's cross where a scene is about to begin. "Let's start over there."

She swallows hard and nods, pulling her shoulders back and pretending to be brave. She's trembling, though, and her skin is pale. I suspect it's taking a tremendous amount of bravery to convince herself to do this. I wonder how many times she debated not showing up in the last few hours. I also wonder why she's here.

I set a hand on the small of her back and guide her toward the cross, leading her to one side where fewer people are gathered. I want to be able to whisper to her without disturbing anyone.

She sets her hands on the half wall. I stand slightly to

one side, as close as I can get to her without touching her. I give half of my attention to the scene in my peripheral vision, but I'm watching Faye. I want to see how she reacts to everything.

The couple performing is well-known to me and everyone in the room. They are married. Faye doesn't know this, though. She has no idea who they are. Matt and Tammy.

Matt whispers in Tammy's ear before lifting her dress over her head and tossing it aside, leaving her naked.

Faye's breath hitches and her eyes widen yet again as her fingers come to her throat to play with the pearls. Somehow, the pearls make her look even more innocent. She's thirty-one years old but looks like she's in her early twenties. Part of that is her skin, but most of it is her innocence.

I thought the nudity might shock her, and it has. I don't think she has blinked since Tammy's body was unveiled. Tammy is a gorgeous woman. She's real. She and Matt have two kids, so she has a soft belly and stretch marks. She earned them, and I know Matt worships them. Her hips are wide from childbirth. Her ass is the perfect handful. Her breasts hang slightly from nursing. Everyone in the club is mesmerized when Tammy performs naked.

I'm unable to look away from Faye. My cock is rock-hard from her expression. It's illogical. I don't understand this hold she has on me. I want to touch her. I don't.

Matt guides Tammy to the cross. He whispers to her again. I know he's giving her directions. He never speaks loud enough for anyone else to hear when they scene. It's as though his instructions are private and only for her to hear, even though everyone watching can surmise what he has said.

Tammy faces the cross and lifts her hands over her head to wrap her fingers around the pegs. Matt knows exactly where to place the pegs to precisely stretch his wife's body how he wants it. He placed them before the scene started.

She spreads her legs at the same time, opening herself up and making herself vulnerable.

Faye licks her lips. The lip gloss she was wearing is almost gone. I wonder if it's flavored. Does she know I'm watching her? I'm not hiding the fact at all. Anyone looking at me must know I'm staring at Faye, though I doubt any of the members are paying attention to me with the Matt-and-Tammy show going on. It's far more alluring.

Matt stands behind his wife and lovingly smooths his hands up her sides from her hips to her breasts. When his fingers stroke the edges of her breasts, she arches her chest forward and tips her head back. She's already in subspace. It's easy for her. Once she turns herself over to her Dom, her entire demeanor changes.

Faye sucks in a breath and holds it, clenching her pearls with her fingers. If she pulls any harder, the necklace will snap, and pearls will ping across the room.

She's so fucking gorgeous, standing there mesmerized by the couple who haven't really done anything yet.

Matt steps closer to his wife, pressing his fully clothed body against her back as he slides his palms around to cup her breasts and then pinch her nipples.

She rises onto her toes, causing him to admonish her. "Feet flat, my pet," he says loud enough for everyone to hear. "You know better."

She moans as she lowers to her heels.

Matt keeps his body against hers as he reaches up to secure first one wrist and then the other to the cross. She will still hold on to the pegs, but if she should try to release them and lower her arms, she will come up short.

Next, Matt squats to the floor and secures her ankles before sliding his palms up her inner thighs, stopping just short of her pussy.

Faye squeezes her legs together. Her mouth is hanging open, but she's not breathing. Her cheeks are flushed a lovely shade of pink. She's turned on, and so am I.

Tammy is panting when Matt steps away. She sways slightly back and forth, anticipating his next move. He doesn't do the same thing every time, so she can't be sure what he will do, but she noticeably squirms when he lowers a blindfold over her eyes.

Faye's fingers release her necklace and trail up to her lips. She absentmindedly rubs them. I want to do the same thing. I want to rub her lips with my fingers and then press my middle finger into her mouth and command her to suck.

Somehow, I know she would do so. With a little training, this gorgeous woman would eagerly drop to her knees, tip her head back, clasp her hands behind her back, and suck my fingers.

The visual is all-consuming. I want to see Faye on her knees, knees wide, hands behind her head, tits raised. I'm nearly salivating.

I broke up with my girlfriend three weeks ago. I'm in no state of mind to entertain the idea of taking a new sub. I shouldn't be lusting after this newbie. It's batshit crazy.

Matt picks up two supple floggers, steps behind his wife, and starts swinging them through the air. He's getting the feel of the rhythm without touching her. After several swings, he steps closer and lets the soft leather gently stroke her shoulder blades.

Tammy moans and tips her head back. She's so sensual.

She's not half as mesmerizing as Faye. The way Faye's stroking her lips makes me nearly groan. She has no fucking clue she's killing me.

When Matt picks up the pace, striking Tammy harder, the thuds landing against her shoulder blades, Faye flinches. Suddenly, she turns to me, lowers her hand, and lifts onto her toes to whisper in my ear.

She doesn't touch me, but her balancing act to avoid doing so is impressive. "Are there rules?"

I know what she's referring to, so when she lowers to her feet, I lean toward her ear. I'm not keeping my hands to myself, though. I set one on the small of her back as I whisper, "Not many. Safe, sane, and consensual. Most Doms will not draw blood. That's why intense impact play is better on naked skin. It helps us ensure we aren't striking too hard."

She turns toward me, grabs my arm this time, and angles her lips to my ear again. "Most Doms? So, sometimes it's okay to draw blood?"

*Not for me.* I force myself not to react. Of all the questions she could ask me, this one lands awfully close to home.

She shivers when I lean in closer than necessary to whisper again, "Occasionally, blood play is permitted. Members need to get it approved by Drake and me first.

That goes for knife play and any other impact play—like a cat o' nine tails. We put extra monitors on scenes that will involve blood. I like to be certain the submissive is fully consenting the entire time."

She nods and resumes watching. Her hands go to the short wall once again, and her knuckles turn white when she grips it.

Matt shifts the floggers to one hand, flattens himself to his wife's back, and cups her neck with his other hand. He tips her head back erotically and whispers in her ear.

Faye turns to me. "What's he saying?" she mouths.

I lean toward her. "He's making sure she's okay. It's important to check in with a submissive during a scene to ensure they're in the right headspace and enjoying themselves."

Matt lowers his hand to Tammy's breast and squeezes it hard.

Tammy moans. She needs the pain. She craves it.

When her husband releases her breast, he slides that hand down to cup her pussy.

Tammy whimpers loudly as she rocks forward.

Faye gives a small gasp as her fingers come to her lips again.

I want to draw her hand away from her mouth and replace it with mine. The desire to order her to suck my fingers is stronger than before. I want to drag her out of this playroom, rush her up to my third-floor apartment, and flatten her against the door so I can ravish her mouth.

I need to take a step back and pull my shit together. I'm not thinking straight.

A throat clearing to my side makes me shift my attention to the left.

It's Asher Bennett. He's one of our most prominent

members with a top-tier membership to the third floor. Drake and I have known him and another of our elite members, Isaac, since college.

Asher keeps his voice low. "Sorry to interrupt. There's a minor incident on the first floor. Drake sent me to get you."

I wince. *Shit.*

Faye glances at me. "I'm fine. Go."

As much as I hate my next words, I look at Asher. "I was giving Faye a tour. It's her first night here. Can you take over for me? This was our first stop."

Asher nods. "No problem. Happy to help."

I force myself not to give him a pointed stare. It's not my place to make decisions for Faye. I don't want to leave her completely alone in the club because she's far too naïve and green to make wise decisions or know who to fully trust.

My members are well-vetted. Drake and I are choosy. We don't allow any nonsense. One strike, and you're out. But some Doms are pushier than others. Faye is a gorgeous woman and is obviously out of her element. I don't want just anyone to swoop in and take her under their wing.

I can trust Asher. He will not take advantage of her or steer her wrong. I wouldn't ask him if I didn't already know he came to the club alone tonight and told me he had no specific plans to scene.

"Thank you." I turn toward Faye. "Asher will answer any questions you have. I'll catch up with you later."

She gives me a smile that doesn't quite reach far enough. She's being brave, but she's not super fond of the idea of me leaving her with a stranger. My chest swells a bit. Good. I'm feeling so fucking possessive of her that it would break me a little if she shrugged me off.

As I jog down the back stairs to the first floor, I take deep breaths and give myself a pep talk. *Shake her off, man. What the hell are you thinking? You're rebounding hard. Do not lure this woman into your web. It's too soon. She's not your type. Remember—women suck.*

# CHAPTER 5

## FAYE

I don't see Easton again for a few hours. I hate that I'm disappointed by that fact, but it's better this way. He was just being nice. I can't let him take up space in my head.

Easton has a commanding presence that lets me know he's a strong Dominant. I bet he has dozens of women vying for his attention every night. I have no idea why he spent as much time with me as he did.

For all I know, he had an arrangement with Asher and asked him to intervene at that precise moment so Easton could extricate himself from me and not get stuck babysitting me all night.

Asher is a firm Dom, too. I know this based on how other members react when passing us. He's extremely polite, though, and never strays from my side. He doesn't permit anyone to lure him away from his babysitting job.

I should be attracted to him. He's a good-looking man. But I'm not interested. Why would I be? I've never found myself interested in any man for more than a fleeting moment. Until Easton.

It's not that I'm not interested in men. I am. I like to look at them. I've just never wanted to do more than look.

Until Easton.

Gah. I need to shake that man out of my system.

Part of my problem is that I don't trust easily. I'm thirty-one years old, and I'm still stuck in the headspace I had in high school. I shudder at the memory of the one time someone asked me out on a date. It was my senior year. A guy I barely knew asked me out for dinner and a movie. After years of being tormented and bullied, I was leery, but he'd been new to the school. I had hoped he hadn't known my reputation as the class dork. So, I accepted. I got all dressed up, fixed my hair, put on makeup, and he never showed.

On Monday, I could hear people whispering and chuckling behind my back. I'd become the biggest joke of the school. The class bullies had gotten their hands on that asshole and convinced him to toy with me. It was one of the most humiliating moments in my life.

I don't let any man get close enough to me so nothing like that can ever happen again. I remind myself of this rule as I take a deep breath and glance at Asher. He's no Easton. I feel nothing for him, but the club has affected me.

Asher has introduced me indirectly to nearly every apparatus in the club. We have stopped for ten or fifteen minutes to watch people performing all over the room. By the time we come back to where I started, I'm a wreck.

I've never been so aroused in my life. I'm shaking from the overload of sex in the air. I haven't watched anyone actually have intercourse, but penis-in-vagina penetration is about the only thing I have not seen tonight.

I'm sure if I wandered around another time, I would be able to check that last thing off my bingo card. I've seen submissives orgasm from being masturbated. I've seen several blow jobs. I've watched women touch themselves. None of that was as jarring as the erections I've seen tonight.

What no one knows is that before tonight, the only penises I've ever seen have been in medical journals. I'm too prissy and worried to pull up images on my computer.

I tried not to react. I didn't want Asher to realize how inexperienced I am. It's embarrassing. What thirty-one-year-old woman hasn't seen or touched a penis?

Asher hasn't said much. Mostly, he has followed me around and let me be still with my thoughts. Now that we've stopped in between apparatuses, he looks directly at me. His expression is serious, brows furrowed. "Is this your first time visiting a kink club?"

"Yes."

"What made you decide to explore this side of yourself?"

I shrug. "I'm not sure I'm really exploring anything about myself. I was just curious. One of my co-workers brought me to the intro class, and I found myself wanting to know more."

His intense gaze makes me tremble. I feel like I'm staring at a shrink, and he's about to dissect me. Analyze me. Tell me things I do not want to hear. "What happened to your friend? Did she join?"

"No. She decided it was too..."

"Kinky?" He chuckles.

"I guess." It hasn't escaped my attention that it's

rather ironic. Trinity dragged me to the intro class, and then she spent the entire ride home shuddering. She pretended to be interested while we were here, but as soon as we got in the car, she blew out a breath and said she couldn't possibly put herself out there like that.

I said nothing. I let her believe I agreed. Intellectually, I did agree. Who *would* put themselves out there like that? In an odd twist, I was the one intrigued, and here I am now. I didn't tell her I was considering coming back, and I'm not sure I'll ever tell her I did. I don't feel like hashing out my reasons with her or anyone.

"What did you learn about yourself?" Asher asks.

"Uh, I don't know." I'm not lying. I have no idea. All I know is that I'm trembling with need. From watching. Maybe I'm a voyeur. Easton said some people like to watch and nothing more. That's certainly a comfortable thought. It requires nothing from me. It doesn't even require me to make myself vulnerable and submit to anyone.

"Would it be presumptuous of me to make an observation?" Asher asks.

My heart rate picks up. I'm nervous to hear what he has to say, but I should probably value his opinion and hear him out. "Go ahead."

"I think the idea of being exposed arouses you."

My breath hitches. My head is spinning. Exposed? Why would I want to be exposed? "Me?"

"Yes, you. It may seem as though you liked to watch others, but I think you were jealous. Not in a bad way, mind you. But that you wished you were them."

"Who?"

"Any submissive who was stripped, either partially or fully. It didn't matter what the Dominant did to them afterward. What mattered was that he let everyone see their breasts or their bottoms or their pussies. If they were forced to become aroused, your reaction was even stronger."

I'm not breathing. My face heats. I can't process what he's telling me. He has to be wrong. Why would I want anyone to see me naked? I've never even been naked in private with anyone, let alone in public.

"Just something to think about." Asher shrugs. "I've been a Dominant for a long time. I'm pretty good at judging submissives. Ponder the idea when you get home. You might consider trying it out. You could do a light scene with someone. Another night, mind you. You're exhausted tonight. I wouldn't do anything rash after all that you've witnessed."

"Who would I do a scene with? You?"

He shakes his head. "Not necessarily. I'm not suggesting you should scene with anyone in particular. Either I, Easton, or Drake could recommend someone if you're interested."

I stare at him, dumbfounded by this information. Seconds tick by.

Suddenly, Easton appears at my side. "I'm so sorry I took so long." He's slightly winded, as if he took the stairs two at a time to get back to me. I'm not sure why.

"It's okay," I murmur.

Asher smiles. "I think she's overloaded with information. We watched damn near every type of scene. It was a busy night tonight."

"Thank you so much for accompanying her," Easton says.

"It was my pleasure. Everything okay on the main floor?"

Easton rolls his eyes and rubs the back of his neck with one hand. "Yes. A couple of drunk people got into it with each other. Broke some glasses. Threw a few punches. Drake and I don't like that shit in our club."

Asher winced. "Shit. Sorry."

"It's over now. We had to revoke four memberships, though. That doesn't happen often." Easton rolls his neck and sighs.

Asher clasps Easton's shoulder in that way men tend to do. "I'm going to get going." He turns toward me. "Nice to meet you, Faye. Enjoy the rest of your evening."

"Thank you," I murmur, feeling awkward. I'm glad he doesn't mention the bomb he dropped before Easton joined us.

"What did you think?" Easton asks as soon as Asher is gone.

"I'm overwhelmed," I respond honestly.

"Understandable. Do you have any questions?"

I shake my head. I have a million questions, but there's no way I can verbalize them right now. Nor do I want to. I'd rather go home and deal with my thoughts on my own. "I should go home. It's late, and I'm exhausted."

"That's normal after your first visit, especially when you're new to the kink community." He lifts a hand, hesitates, and then gently touches my cheek before pulling away. It's kind of sweet and unexpected. Now, I have more questions. "You have my number. Call or text if you have any questions. Your membership is covered for a month. We're open Wednesday through Saturday, eight to two. Come as often as you'd like."

"Thank you." When I turn toward the door leading back to the reception area, he follows me.

"Are you okay to drive?"

"Oh, yes. I'll be fine. I didn't drink anything." I never drink alcohol. I don't like the taste, and even the thought of feeling out of control makes me shudder. I really am a prude.

But am I? I'm shook by Asher's suggestion. He thinks I want to be exposed? It's ludicrous, isn't it?

"Alcohol isn't the only type of impairment you might have when you leave Edge, Faye," Easton informs me as he continues to follow me into the locker room. "Have you heard of sub drop?"

I shake my head as I pull my purse and coat out of my locker.

Easton takes my coat from me and helps me into it like a gentleman. He even adjusts my jacket on my shoulders and zips it up before gripping my biceps and meeting my gaze again. "Sub drop is what sometimes happens to a submissive after a scene. It's real, and you should take it seriously. It can also happen just from watching. You watched a lot tonight."

He narrows his gaze and stares at me as if trying to decide if I look safe to drive.

"I'm fine. I promise."

"Okay, but don't be surprised if you feel lethargic or overly tired tomorrow. It's normal after an endorphin high. You've experienced an adrenaline rush. When it subsides, you may feel almost hungover."

I lick my lips. "Okay." It seems preposterous, but I'm listening.

"Be careful driving home." He hesitates and then speaks again. "Would you mind texting me when you get home so I'll know you made it safely?"

I nod. "Okay."

He smiles. "Thank you. I don't mean to overstep, but it's your first night, and I'm worried."

"I'll text you."

He releases me and guides me to the steps. "Someone at the entrance will walk you to your car. Don't go alone."

I nod again. That's quite the service, but I guess this isn't some hole-in-the-wall bar. It's a private club with a significant membership fee.

As soon as I step into the stairwell, leaving Easton behind, I feel a weird letdown. Was that what he was talking about? I think in my case it's just that I'm sorry to be leaving.

I have a lot to think about.

# CHAPTER 6

EASTON

"How'd it go with Faye?" Drake asks me when I drop into my chair in my office fifteen minutes later. I'm in a sour mood because I wasn't the one to show her around the club. It took two hours to fucking deal with the drunk-and-disorderly issue downstairs.

I own this club with Drake, and sometimes, we have no choice but to deal with problems, but why the fuck did tonight have to be one of those nights? And why do I care? I should be grateful I was called away. I should also be grateful it was Asher I was able to leave Faye with. He's one of the best.

If I had remained with her all evening, I might have ended up saying or doing something inappropriate. She's not my type, I remind myself, and I'm not interested in a new relationship.

*Keep telling yourself that.*

"Asher showed her around," I say.

Drake winces. "Sorry about that."

I shrug. "Sorry about what?" I ask, pretending not to care.

Drake lifts both brows and leans back in his chair. "How long have we known each other?"

I chuckle. This is a line both of us have used our entire lives when one of us tries to lie to the other. We used to respond with quips about sharing a womb and even a sac. Or we would go back further and point out that, technically, we were the same egg and the same sperm. We're identical twins, and we share a unique bond that often includes an eerie sensation that we know things we did not say out loud.

I spin my chair to face him head-on. "Look. You can stop hounding me about Faye. I'm well aware of her presence and my unwanted feelings. Yes, she's fucking gorgeous. Yes, I'm attracted to her. But I just got out of a relationship. I don't need a rebound."

He laughs. "It's been three weeks since you called it off. Besides, things between you and Bethany had been going downhill for months. You knew it wasn't right long before you broke up."

"Doesn't mean I'm ready to jump into something new. I need time."

Drake rolls his eyes. "You're going to have to come up with a better excuse than that."

"Sure. I have a long list. Let's start with how green she is. I don't like to train submissives. I've never liked it. That's why I don't do it. I can't even be sure Faye is definitely submissive. She's exploring. Women who are exploring their kinky side are not my type."

Drake leans forward, setting his elbows on his knees. "I saw you with her before we got called downstairs.

Every inch of your body was a millimeter from hers. You couldn't have gotten any closer to her without touching her if you'd tried. And Faye? She was trembling from watching that scene. Anyone could have seen that at a glance. She could barely control herself. She's so obviously submissive it's like a flashing neon sign above her head."

I sigh. He's probably right, and he's certainly more objective than me.

"As for your rule about not training submissives, you just might have to break it this time. I don't think you'll be able to turn her over to another Dom. What are you going to do when she comes in next weekend and asks you to set her up with someone? Who are you going to choose? Me? Asher? Perhaps Dane or Isaac?"

I wince. He's right. I lean back farther in my chair and run a hand through my hair. "I don't know. Maybe she just wants to watch."

Drake shakes his head. "You didn't get a chance to talk to Asher before he left, did you?"

"No." I stiffen. "What did he say?"

"He said he thinks she might be a bit of an exhibitionist."

My eyes bug out. "Seriously?" The man did spend more time with her than I did, but...exhibitionism? How could he have deduced that?

Drake nods. "Asher is observant, and he's usually spot on. Apparently, she was repeatedly turned on by scenes that involved exposing the submissive, either partially or completely. It didn't matter what the scene was or the apparatus. She clenched in on herself and held her breath when breasts and pussies were exposed."

I think about his words. I only watched the one scene

with her, but that did happen. I wouldn't make the over-generalization from one scene, but perhaps if I had spent the next two hours with her, I would have come to the same conclusion.

"She seems so innocent," I murmur.

"How innocent can she be? She's what? Thirty-one?"

"Yes, but something tells me she's only had extremely vanilla relationships. I'm betting she's been bored to tears in bed. She probably hasn't had an orgasm with a man."

Drake chuckles. "Well, you can certainly fix that."

I roll my eyes. "Rebounding, remember? And I don't do newbies."

He laughs harder and turns toward the computer just as my phone buzzes in my pocket.

I pull it out and smile to see the incoming text from Faye.

> I made it home. Thank you for making me feel welcome. I think my curiosity is satisfied.

I read the text several times. It almost sounds like she's insinuating she doesn't plan to return. I finally text her back.

> I'm glad you made it home safely. Will I see you again next weekend?

Seconds tick by. I turn toward my desk, set the phone down upright, and pretend to be engrossed in something on my computer. I can't focus on a damn thing, though. I want a response.

After ten minutes, when I'm about to pull my hair out and contemplate calling her—which is a horrible idea—I finally get another incoming text.

I don't know. It was overwhelming. I'll think about it.

I draw in a deep breath, grateful when Drake stands and leaves the room. I don't want to hash this out with him. I type a response and then stare at it for a long time. Should I send it? I'm probably making a gigantic mistake, but I can't help myself.

Meet me for coffee tomorrow morning. I'll help you work through your experience. I'm worried you don't have anyone to talk to about this topic, and you're going to rely on the internet for answers.

Another eternal length of time passes. I assume Faye is a very careful person, and she's thinking this through thoroughly before she responds. It's after midnight. The club is still open for two more hours, but I suspect Faye is going to conk out soon. I hope she responds before then.

Finally, another text.

I don't drink coffee... But I'll take you up on your offer. You're right. There is no one I would tell about my experience tonight. Also, I'm very bad at reading people and doubly so in text. Are you being kind to me as a concerned club owner? Or is this a date?

I draw in a breath and find myself grinning even though I hate having to answer her. She's forcing me to be in or out. Can I straddle the line?

> Can we perhaps not define it? We don't know each other very well. I feel drawn to you both as a concerned club owner and as a man, but I'm cautious about labeling things. Is eleven o'clock okay? There's a coffee shop two blocks from you that has a variety of beverages and amazing pastries.

I hope she isn't jarred by the fact that I know where she lives. I'm staring at the information she filled out earlier this evening. I also hope I'm being pushy enough to convince her to meet me without making her feel like I'm ordering her to.

> The Grind. I know the place. I'll be there.

I blow out a long, relieved breath.

> Sleep well, Faye. See you in the morning.

I hope I'm not making the most colossal mistake of my life. Faye is not a woman to toy with. She's brilliant and educated and, I suspect, serious. I don't want to hurt her. I have no explanation for why I want to see her again in eleven hours, but I do. The thought of simply waiting for her to consider coming to Edge again next weekend doesn't sit well with me. Perhaps if we spend some time together outside the club, I can either flush her out of my system or solidify my feelings and give up the fight.

Drake is going to have a field day with this.

# CHAPTER 7

FAYE

I'm a ridiculous ball of nerves as I arrive at The Grind. I'm ten minutes early because I'm always early for everything. I'm going to feel awkward waiting for Easton to arrive, but I would feel more awkward if I were late.

When I step inside, I'm surprised to find he beat me there. He smiles and stands at a table in the far corner of the room.

My heart is racing as I approach him. This is not the sort of thing I do. I don't meet men for coffee. I don't meet men for anything. I don't even understand why I agreed to this.

When I asked him if this was a date or not, I had no idea what I wanted the answer to be. His non-answer had been interesting, and I've tried not to ponder it too much.

Easton reaches out to cup my elbow and air kiss my cheek as soon as I reach him. He did that last night, too.

It's sweet, but it leaves me unnerved. It seems everything leaves me unnerved.

"I'm glad you came, Faye," he says as he pulls out a chair for me. He helps me sit and pushes me closer to the table before resuming his seat. He slides a menu in front of me. "The waitress brought us waters, but I'll give you time to look over the menu."

I bite my lip and lower my gaze, staring at nothing. I know exactly what I'm going to order. I perused the menu before I went to bed last night.

"Did you sleep okay?" he asks.

I lift my head. "Yes. Thank you."

He leans forward, narrows his gaze, and scrutinizes me. After a moment, he gives me a strange, sexy smile. "I'm pretty good at reading people, Faye. I'm also pretty good at restricting my Dominant inclinations to the club, my home, and other private places. However, I'm going to have to put my Dom hat on for a moment and call bull-shit." One brow lifts.

I swallow hard as I stare at him. I'm trembling now. Nerves are eating me alive. I consider fleeing. I could just get up and walk out the door. I could tell him I've changed my mind if I want to be more polite.

Instead, I'm trapped by his stare. I can't look away. It feels like he's commanding me to look at him.

"Let's start over," he says softly. He's not mad. He might even be amused. It's so weird. "Don't tell me what you think I want to hear or what you think is socially appropriate. Answer me truthfully. Did you sleep well?"

I slowly shake my head. I tossed and turned all night. I was worried about meeting him, and I couldn't get the hundreds of things I saw last night out of my mind. "No," I whisper.

He gives me a broader smile. "Good girl. I would have been surprised to find you bright-eyed and bushy-tailed. You had an intense evening. I'm sure you have a million questions. That's why I asked you to meet me."

"Do you ask all new members to meet you for coffee the next morning?" I feel proud of myself for voicing this thought.

He chuckles. "No. I've never met a new member for coffee before."

"Then why are you here with me?" I push.

"I don't completely know, Faye. That's the honest truth. I'm here because I want to be. That's all I know. I promise to be as honest as possible with you."

"Okay."

"What about you? Do you want to be here?"

I nod. "Yes."

He grins. "Perfect. Then we are two people meeting for beverages because it felt like a good idea."

I draw in a breath and let it out slowly.

"Do you know what you want? You hardly looked at the menu." He points toward the laminated page in front of me.

"I already know. I mean, I looked at the menu last night," I admit.

He smiles again. "A woman who likes to be prepared. What did you decide last night?"

"I planned three options," I tell him.

"I'm intrigued. What were they?"

He's oddly easy to talk to. It's unexpected, and I don't know why I'm sharing my quirk with him. I lick my lips. "Well, I figured I would order just green tea if my stomach was too tied in knots to swallow more than that."

He nods, listening intently, unfazed by my admission that I might be sitting here wound up in a tight ball of nerves. "Makes sense. What was option two?"

"Herbal tea and a cherry-filled pastry if I thought I could maybe eat but was still on the fence."

"And lastly?" he encourages.

"Black tea and a ham, egg, and cheese croissant if I could overcome my nerves enough to eat an actual meal."

He reaches across the table and sets his hand on top of mine. "I hope I can make you feel settled enough to eat more than a nibble, and I'm in no hurry. Let's go with option three...? I'll order coffee and a sandwich. We can get a sweet pastry to share."

I realize I'm biting my lip and release it as I nod. "Okay."

A waitress shows up. "Welcome to The Grind. My name is Brynn. Are you ready to order?"

I'm surprised and relieved when Easton orders for both of us. He orders the same sandwich as me, coffee for himself, black tea for me, and the cherry pastry.

Throughout this entire process, his hand is on top of mine, holding me just enough to make me feel grounded. I'm grateful because it seems like I might float off the chair and up toward the ceiling if he lets go.

"Thank you," I murmur when the waitress walks away.

"It's my pleasure." He gives my hand a squeeze before turning it over and threading our fingers together.

I stare at our connection. It feels nice. In the back of my head, I'm worried I'm not being fully honest with him. If this is a date, he is seriously lacking in information about me.

"Look at me, Faye."

I lift my gaze.

"Take a breath."

I inhale and release it slowly.

"Good girl. No pressure. We're just having brunch." He strokes the back of my hand with his thumb.

It feels so nice. I'm warm. I'm so far out of my element.

"Tell me your primary concerns right this moment." He has a way of commanding me subtly.

I shiver.

"Don't overthink it. Just tell me what's on your mind."

"The list is long."

He smiles. "That's okay. Do you have to be anywhere this afternoon?"

"Uh..." I think about my regular Saturday routine and how it's gone out the window. It's all unnecessary, anyway. I don't *have* to clean my bathroom, read my science magazine for thirty minutes while I eat lunch, or iron my shirts for the week. That last one causes me some stress, and I find my mind wandering to when I'll get that task done.

"Faye..."

"I don't need to be anywhere."

"Good. Now, I can sense you're uncomfortable, but I don't think I'm specifically the cause. Am I right?"

I nod. Is he psychic? I feel like he's capable of guessing everything I'm thinking, and it's unnerving.

"When was the last time you went on a date?"

*Shit.* I don't usually cuss, and it was only in my head, but I'm cornered now. I stare at him. I can't lie, and I can't possibly tell him the truth either. He'd run from the bakery.

We're sitting at a quaint round table. The bottom is white iron, and the top is glass. Easton reaches with his free hand and pulls my chair closer to his. "Allow me to withdraw that question. It was too personal. I shouldn't have asked it. Can you share some of your thoughts with me if I promise not to try to control and direct the narrative?" He grins again.

I inhale deeply. I might as well be upfront with him. If he's interested in me, he needs to know I'm an odd bird. I can do this. "I don't date. I'm too awkward. I mostly only focus on my work because I'm introverted and find it difficult to discuss most topics outside of biology. Also, I'm a type A. I used to think I had OCD, but I've realized I'm just more orderly and organized than other people."

He listens intently, never looking away or in any way indicating he thinks I'm a freak. "Thank you for sharing. I know that was hard."

"Maybe you should tell me what you're thinking, too," I suggest. "It's only fair."

He chuckles. "You're right. What you should know about me is that three weeks ago, right before I met you, I broke up with a woman I'd been dating for six months. I had no intention of entertaining the thought of dating another woman so soon, but I'm intrigued by you, and I can't seem to stop thinking about you."

I bite my lip. He can't stop thinking about me? At least it's not just me.

"In full disclosure," he continues, "I also do *not* date women who are not well-versed in the BDSM community. I have very strong Dominant tendencies. It's been many years since I've dated anyone who wasn't certain they were submissive and knew exactly what they wanted out of a D/s relationship. Dominant and submissive, that is."

My shoulders involuntarily drop.

Easton grips my fingers tighter and leans in closer. "I can't explain why I feel compelled to throw caution to the wind and break all my rules with you, but I do."

"Why?" I sit taller. "I don't even know if I'm submissive at all, and I can't possibly tell you what I might like or not like."

He holds my gaze for a while, releasing my hand when the waitress arrives with our plates. As soon as she sets everything on the table, Easton glances at her. "Thank you, Brynn."

"You're most welcome. Enjoy."

When she's gone, Easton grabs my hand again and lifts my chin with his other fingers. "Here's the thing. You're intrigued, which means you're going to come back to my club. You're going to want to do more than watch. You're going to want to experiment. That means I'll be faced with two choices. Either I arrange for you to scene with another Dom, or I introduce you to the pleasures of the kink world myself. The thought of anyone else helping you find yourself makes me want to punch a hole in the drywall. I can't do it. The next time you come to Edge, you will be there as my guest. My submissive. If you want to experiment, you'll do so under my guidance."

I squeeze my thighs together, grateful I chose to wear jeans but wincing because he can see my every move through the glass table top.

He sucks in a breath and winces. "Shit. I told myself I would not pressure you or dominate you this morning, but I just blew that out of the water. I'm sorry."

His discomfort is oddly reassuring to me. This time, I

squeeze his hand. "It's okay. To be honest, if I decide to come back to the club, I wouldn't want anyone besides you to teach me about the kink world."

He gives my hand another squeeze and releases it. "Please accept my apologies for railroading you. I don't know how to be anything but Dominant. Casùal vanilla acquaintances are not in my comfort zone."

"Apology accepted." I feel oddly lighter. I'm not the only one at this table with insecurities. His might look entirely different from mine, but he's still a fish out of water with me, and that makes me feel like I'm on more even ground with him.

He nods toward the sandwiches. "Let's eat. Tell me about your pharmaceutical work while we eat."

I smile. "You googled me."

"Yep."

"I googled you, too, Mr. Technology." I take a bite of my sandwich, surprised by my ability to chew and swallow. I know Easton and his brother, Drake, are computer geniuses who have made millions.

I tell him a bit about my work, and he shares a bit about what he and Drake are working on now. They own the club, and it makes a lot of money, but it's only open four nights a week from eight to two. The rest of the week, those two men bump heads and come up with new concepts.

I'm surprised when I look down and realize I've finished my sandwich and watch as Easton cuts a bite from the cherry pastry sitting between us. There's something intimate about sharing food off a plate. I've never experienced it before.

My breath hitches, and I lift my gaze to his when he offers me the first bite, holding out his fork.

As I lean forward and open my mouth, I squeeze my legs together again. Why does it seem so erotic to take a bite off his fork?

He smiles as I savor the bite, still holding his gaze. "Mmm."

"Is it good?" he asks.

"Delicious."

He feeds me another bite and reaches across to wipe the corner of my lips with his thumb. "Powdered sugar," he whispers.

My cheeks heat as I swallow and take a sip of my tea. "Aren't you going to eat some?"

"It's more fun watching you eat. Besides, I feel like I know exactly how good it is from watching your expressions."

My heart rate picks up. How does he manage to make it sound like we just had sex instead of sharing a pastry?

He takes the next bite and moans around it. "You're right. It's delicious."

I find myself disappointed when it's all gone. We have no reason to continue sitting here. We'll part ways now, and the rest of my day will seem boring. The rest of my *life* will seem boring. He's ruining me.

When the waitress brings the bill, Easton drops more than enough cash under it on the table and faces me. "It's nice out today. We should take advantage of the warmer weather and slight sunshine. What do you think about heading over to the Olympic Sculpture Park? We can wander, take in the views, and enjoy the artwork."

"I love the Olympic Sculpture Park. I haven't been there in a while." I sit taller. He doesn't want to end this date. I'm a combination of relieved and nervous. He's easy to be with, even though I'm awkward. He doesn't notice or mind or care, I guess.

"Good. It's decided then." He stands, holds out a hand, and helps me to my feet. "Will you be warm enough?"

I'm wearing jeans, a navy sweater, and tennis shoes. I had no idea what to wear this morning, but I finally decided to go with comfort. Now I'm glad. "I think so. It's warmer than usual today."

Easton keeps one hand on the small of my back as he guides me out of the bakery and over to a sleek black sports car parked on the street. He opens the passenger door for me, helps me in, and makes sure I'm settled before shutting the door and jogging to his side.

I've done a lot of research on BDSM, but I don't know a thing about how Dominants behave outside of the club environment. Easton is a total gentleman.

After he climbs in his side, he reaches all the way across me. I'm confused for a moment before I realize he has pulled my seatbelt over my body. He buckles it, saying nothing, and then taps my nose. "Ready?"

I'm so out of my element. I've never been on a date before. I've never been in a car with a man. This is definitely a date—and Easton is definitely a man. I nod.

I'm at a loss for words as he drives through the city, eventually pulling into the parking garage for the park. He pays the parking fee and finds a spot.

After quickly rounding the car again, he helps me out. This time, I at least think to remove the seatbelt, though maybe I should have left it and let him do it. He would have had to bend really close to me again to unbuckle me.

He locks the car and takes my hand, but instead of leading me away from the car, he turns me, leans me against the passenger door, and sets his palms on my shoulders.

His body is fully aligned with mine. He's so close, he's almost pressing against me. His hands slide to my neck, and he tips my head back with his thumbs.

Everything this man does exudes dominance. Does he know it? Probably.

# CHAPTER 8

## FAYE

I hold my breath as I look into his eyes. Is he going to kiss me?

He sets his forehead against mine and growls. "You've bewitched me, Faye. I thought if we had coffee together in a vanilla setting, I would realize we aren't the least bit compatible. Instead, you've lured me in deeper. I want to kiss you senseless while I slide my hand between your legs and rub your pussy until you come hard in your jeans."

I gasp. My entire body trembles. I think I could come any second from listening to his words. I'm panting.

He growls again. "Every time you react to me with those innocent doe eyes, I fall harder under your spell. I want to own you. I want to mold you and train you to submit to me. I've never worked with someone as green as you. I don't train submissives. I don't have the patience for it. But then you stepped into my club, and

73

now I want things I've never wanted before. I want to erase every previous experience you've had with any man. I feel sort of violent about it. Possessive. It's irrational how jealous I am of every previous boyfriend you've had."

My lips part. It's hard to concentrate. He's scrambling my brain. My breasts feel heavy, and he's standing so close that my nipples are rubbing against his chest through my sweater and bra.

Easton is breathing heavily, and I think he's struggling to control himself as he lowers his face to my neck and nuzzles me below my ear. "You smell amazing," he whispers.

His scent fills *my* nose, too. It's calming. Almost familiar. I tip my head to the side, giving him better access. God, I want him to kiss me.

He licks my earlobe and bites it just enough to make me whimper. He growls again. "What are you doing to me, woman?"

I don't have an answer, and I don't think he needs one. But I'm scared out of my mind. I could easily let him consume me, and when this thing is over, I'm going to get hurt.

But I can't stop it either. I want this experience. I want to know what it feels like to be with a man. I'm not stupid enough to think we would become a couple or anything. Like he said, we aren't compatible. I'm a very awkward, dorky, inexperienced fish out of water. He's this buff, sexy, confident Dominant.

I don't know why he's so intrigued by me, but I do know it can't last. Do I take a chance anyway and let him take me places I never thought I would go? I can't turn this around now. It's too late. I'd regret it for the rest of my life. I'll take this opportunity and figure out how to pick up the pieces afterward.

I lift my hands to his waist and hold on to the loops of his jeans.

"I love how you tremble in my arms," he whispers in my ear.

I shiver every time his breath hits my neck. A soft moan escapes my lips. He's making it impossible to think. I'm vaguely aware that we're standing in a parking garage. Anyone who walks by can see us in this intimate embrace. It's so erotic, and I don't care.

"Tell me you're going to let me train you, Faye," he murmurs.

I bite my lip. I'm going to let him do whatever he wants with me. I know it in my soul. I can fight it, but I can't stop it.

He lifts his head from my neck, cups my face with both hands, and holds my gaze from two inches away. His body is leaning into mine. His expression is so intense. "Let me be the one, Faye. Let me teach you everything you need to know about BDSM. Let me help you find your authentic kink."

I nod. There's no other option.

He gives me a slow smile. "God, you're so fucking sexy. When I look into your eyes, I see tremendous innocence. It's irrational. It's hot as fuck."

I lick my lips. "It's not irrational," I mutter.

He searches my gaze, shifting his attention from one eye to the other over and over. "How many men have you slept with, Faye?"

I swallow hard. Will he stuff me back in this car and take me home if I tell him the truth?

"Faye..."

I draw in a breath. "None."

He hesitates for a moment, and then his eyes pop wide.

I'm freaking out inside. He's going to release me any second as though I've burned him.

"You're a virgin?"

My cheeks heat further. I say nothing.

"Jesus..." He doesn't release me. In fact, his hands are tighter on my face, his body pressing harder against me. His forehead comes to mine again, and he closes his eyes, taking deep breaths.

I want to know what he's thinking, but I don't move or speak. I wait. This confrontation was inevitable. Better to get it out of the way now. If he's going to end this thing before it starts, at least I won't be left shredded and destroyed.

That's probably not true. I would already be shredded if he changed his mind. I'll understand. Who wants to date a woman as weird and inexperienced as me? I won't blame him. But I will probably spend the rest of the weekend in a fetal position, trying to pull myself together.

He licks his lips, opens his eyes, and leans his head back again. Inches. Not more. "How many men have touched your pussy?"

I flinch at the crude word. I won't lie to him. He's trying to make a decision. "None."

"How many have suckled your breasts?"

"None." I'm going to pass out from the stress of this.

"How many men have you kissed?"

"None."

"No one has touched you? Ever?"

I glance to the right and then the left when his voice raises. "Maybe you could shout that a bit louder. I don't think the people in the skyscrapers heard you." I'm never sarcastic. I don't even know where those words come from. I'm embarrassed. This is humiliating. I'd rather he strip me naked next to the car than tell everyone in earshot I'm a virgin.

He winces and looks around. "Fuck. I'm sorry. I wasn't thinking."

No one is nearby. No one heard him. I doubt he was as loud as it sounded in my head.

He slides his thumbs to my mouth and strokes.

I part my lips, breathing heavily.

He stares at my lips. "Last night, you kept touching your lips, and I desperately wanted to stroke them myself. I kept visualizing you letting my fingers into your mouth and sucking on them." His voice is low and gravelly.

Some Faye from a parallel universe flicks her tongue out and licks his thumb. I don't know her, but I like how bold she is.

His breath hitches. "Faye..." He eases his thumbs away from my lips.

"Are you going to take me home now?"

His brows furrow. "Why would I do that?"

I shrug. "You can date any woman in the universe. Surely, you'd rather it not be someone as ignorant about everything as I am."

His eyes widen. "Oh, baby, you are sorely mistaken. I'm so turned on right now I'm going to come in my pants. Inside, I'm doing a weird, ugly, happy dance with fists pumping. All of your firsts will be mine. That does not turn me off."

I purse my lips. He seems sincere.

"Here's what we're going to do," he declares, seemingly pulling himself together. "First, if it's okay with you,

I'm going to kiss you. Then, I'm going to take your hand, and we're going to enjoy the Olympic Sculpture Park for a few hours. After that, I'm going to take you shopping. After that, we'll go to dinner. Next, we'll go to Edge. We'll go before it opens so I can spend some time showing you around the club with no one watching. If you're up to it, we can do a scene together, either in private before people arrive, in a private room, or in front of the other members."

"Uhh...I got stuck back on the kissing part, and most of the rest was a blur," I admit.

He chuckles. "Let's do that first then. Yeah?"

"You won't judge me?"

"Never. Not about anything. I will cherish every first you let me have. Even if you only give me this one, I will forever hold it in my heart."

"You're very confusing," I say, frowning.

"How's that?" He's grinning.

"Half the time, you talk like you're going to boss me around and bend me to your will. The other half of the time, you act like you're going to give me choices."

He winces, but he's still grinning at the same time. "That's because I keep forgetting how green you are. The Dom in me wants to control everything. Then I remember you aren't familiar with how a D/s relationship works. The most important thing for you to understand is that you hold all of the power in everything we do. Nothing happens without your consent."

I frown, confused. "I don't understand a word of what you just said."

"It's a power exchange, Faye. Every inch of me wants you to turn that power over to me. But it's yours to give. Not mine to take. You have to give me permission to dominate you. Safe, sane, and consensual. We'll gradually talk through the aspects of what a D/s relationship looks like, but every step of the way, I will make sure you're consenting. My goal is to give you exactly what you need and not one ounce more. I have no interest in pushing someone to do something that doesn't make them squirm. I want you to crave what we do together. I want you trembling with need. If anything feels off or you're not ready for it, I will back up. You will learn to use a safeword."

"Okay." I'm not sure I fully grasp this rabbit hole I've fallen into, but hopefully, he will repeat everything later.

"Your eyes are glassy. Don't worry. I will explain everything as we go along."

Is he still going to kiss me? I look at his lips.

"I guess you're okay with the idea of me kissing you," he teases as his lips come to my cheek. His hands slide down to my shoulders.

"Yes, please."

He growls again. I like that sound. It makes me feel sexy.

He kisses my cheek and then nibbles a path to my lips. At first, he's careful and tentative, kissing me gently and slowly. It's nice, but I like it better when he angles his head to one side and deepens the kiss. His lips part, and he licks along the seam of my mouth until I open for him.

When his tongue slides along my bottom lip, I grip his belt loops tighter. Who knew a kiss could be so arousing? I moan when he slides his tongue against mine and then gently sucks mine into his mouth.

So, this is kissing... It doesn't seem like any kiss I've ever seen in real life or on TV. It's so much more. I'm leaning into him. I feel wanton and desperate. I never want it to end.

Easton groans into my mouth as he continues to devour me as though I'm his last meal. It's so erotic. If anyone is watching, they're getting an eyeful. I hope there are no kids around.

It seems like an hour before he releases my mouth. He's panting. "Faye..." His voice is reverent. I think he's pleased. "You're going to ruin me."

That's interesting since I was already thinking *he* was going to ruin *me*.

# CHAPTER 9

## EASTON

I don't remember when I've had this much fun with a woman. I even managed to keep our day together as vanilla as possible after the intense way I basically claimed Faye like some kind of wolf shifter against my car.

That's basically how I feel. Like an animal following some ritualistic pheromones or some shit. She's like a drug.

While we were at the Olympic Sculpture Park, she loosened up. I caught her smiling genuinely several times. She's a curious sponge and wanted to read about each sculpture as we passed them. I finally had to drag her back to the car with promises that we would come again soon and see more.

I think part of the reason she didn't want to leave was because she was nervous about my shopping plans—and rightfully so—because the next place we went was an upscale fetish shop called Kink Outfitters. I know the owner, Barbara, and I texted her ahead to let her know I was bringing in someone important to me, warning her that Faye was also as green as they come so she would be prepared.

Barbara understood perfectly and was very lowkey and helpful. I sat on the loveseat outside the fitting rooms and let Barbara do her thing. It was difficult because I really would have preferred dressing and undressing Faye myself, but we're not there yet by any stretch.

In addition, the two women ganged up on me and decided I wouldn't even get a single glimpse of what they chose. That frustrated me. I really, really wanted Faye to come out and let me see what she was trying on, but she refused, and Barbara supported her.

When we left the shop with a sealed black bag in the back seat of my car, we went to an early dinner at my favorite Italian restaurant. I gave Faye the name of the place when we got in the car. After listening to what she'd gone through last night deciding what to eat this morning at The Grind, I realized she would be more comfortable upon arrival if she made her selection while still in the car.

I enjoyed glancing at her while she perused the online menu, noting how she chewed on the bottom corner of her lip, contemplating what she would order as if she were choosing a tattoo that would be permanently inked on her skin.

My next thought was even more disturbing. My Dom decided there was no way I would ever permit Faye to get a tattoo. I haven't even seen most of her body yet, but I'm confident she doesn't have any tattoos, and she's never getting one.

I know I'm a strong Dom. I've known it for many years. I don't usually surprise myself, but the level of control I feel like I want to have over this woman is far beyond anything I've ever experienced with any prior submissive. I've never even had a long-term girlfriend I felt this possessive of.

It's scary as fuck because I don't have permission to dominate Faye like I crave. She isn't educated enough in the kink world to turn that kind of power over to me. And then there's the fact that I've been single for only three weeks. I have no business jumping into another relationship of any sort, let alone one that's as deep as this one is portending to be.

I did not take Faye back to her place after dinner, even though she made that request. I didn't tell her why because I didn't want to freak her out further, but the truth is I was afraid if we went into her apartment, we would not make it to the club.

I don't absolutely have to be at Edge tonight. I could have called Drake and told him I wouldn't be there. We have plenty of employees, and we sometimes manage without both of us there.

I've made a promise to myself, and I intend to keep it. I will keep my pants on tonight. Lord knows I want to be inside Faye more than I've ever wanted to be inside anyone. But it's too soon. I'm bombarding her with far too much. I won't also claim her virginity while she's dealing with understanding her submission.

I have no right to take that from her. It would be a bastard move. It's mindboggling that she's gone thirty-one years without having sex, and I will not be a cocky asshole about it. Faye deserves to be in a more committed relationship before she lets a man get that close to her pussy.

I'm not sure I have the willpower to *never* touch her, and I certainly don't have thoughts of entering a committed relationship with *any* woman. Nevertheless, it's likely I will eventually claim every inch of her, but not tonight.

We arrive at Edge at six-thirty, and Faye becomes quiet and fidgety as I help her out of the car. I grab the bag from the back seat and lead her inside. The first floor is silent at this time. Employees will start arriving at seven, but even Drake isn't here this early.

I lead Faye up to the second floor, hesitate, and then take her hand and turn toward the door leading to the third floor. I type my code into the keypad to disengage the lock and open the door on the landing before guiding her up another flight. We have an elevator, but I rarely use it. I'm glad we installed it, though, because it comes in handy when we need to move equipment to the third floor.

"What's on the third floor?" she asks.

"Our highest-tiered membership is for the third floor," I explain. "You'll see."

"There's another membership level above the one for five hundred dollars a month?"

"Yep." I don't elaborate. I would blow her mind.

I pause at the third-floor office I share with Drake. "Drake and I often sit in here when the club is open."

"Wow. That's a lot of monitors. How can you possibly watch them all at once?" she asks as she steps inside.

"We have another room with the same monitors downstairs and several employees who watch them closely."

She looks around at each of them. They're on, but

there's no one in the building besides us, so nothing interesting is happening.

"Come." I give her hand a tug and nod over my shoulder. "Let me show you my private space."

She silently follows me out of the office and into my private play space.

I release her hand as she wanders in. As I shut and lock the door behind me, I realize bringing her here is not better than if I had brought her to her apartment. We're alone. Hell, we're alone no matter where we go in the club, but in this particular space, we're extremely alone.

Faye crosses her arms as she slowly moves around the room. "This is yours?"

"Yes. Each top-tiered member has their own little studio apartment like this on the third floor. They can bring a guest up here anytime they want. No one is permitted to live here, but they can stay overnight if they don't abuse the privilege. It's not meant to be a place to live. Each apartment has a mini fridge, a microwave, a bed, and an attached bathroom, but it's not meant to be someone's home. It's not an issue. No one who can afford the membership for this floor is hurting for rent money."

"I don't think I even want to know how much that membership is," she murmurs.

Probably not. So I don't tell her.

"You bring women here and dominate them?" She steps closer to my spanking bench, but as she trails her fingers over it, her gaze is on the king-sized bed that is covered with black satin sheets and a silky black comforter. It has four posts, and each post has various rings at different heights so I can restrain a submissive.

"Yes." I watch her draw in a breath. "Don't get me wrong. I don't bring women here every night or anything.

The only person who's been in this room in almost a year was Bethany, my ex, and that didn't happen often as our relationship came to an end because we didn't see eye-to-eye with regard to her submission."

Faye turns toward me. "What does that mean?"

I clear my throat. Faye deserves to know the answer to anything she wants to ask. I need to be an open book. "Bethany wanted to submit to me on a deeper level than I was willing to give her. We couldn't agree. We argued about it often. I rarely brought her to this room as things went south between us. Hell, I rarely brought her to the club at all for the past two months. I didn't want to fight."

Faye stares at me. "She wanted to submit to you deeper than you were willing? I'm not following. You seem pretty Dominant to me."

"She wanted me to hurt her," I explain.

Faye blinks.

"I wouldn't do it. I've never hurt a submissive in my life. I won't even spank someone without their skin bare so I can monitor how the impact from my palm is affecting them."

"I can't grasp that," Faye whispers. "Someone wanting more than that, I mean."

"To be honest, I can't either. It's not entirely uncommon for people to do a scene on the second floor that involves breaking the skin. They have to request permission, and Drake and I are careful about who we grant that permission to, but sometimes people like to be struck so hard they bleed or end up with deep bruises. It's just not my kink."

Faye shudders before hugging herself. "Well, that's good to know."

I stay where I am near the door. I haven't moved since

we entered the room. I don't want her to feel threatened. "Nothing will happen between us that we don't negotiate first, Faye. It will seem like all we ever do is negotiate for a while because every time we do something new, we'll discuss it ahead of time. Once we're in an active scene, I will never introduce something that we have not discussed. You have my word. Not even if you ask me. When you're submitting to me, it is not the time to change the rules. You can't consent while you're in that headspace."

"Okay."

I wander to the loveseat and sit on one end. "Will you sit with me?"

She joins me, unfolding her arms as she sits so she can rub her palms on her thighs.

Fuck, but she has me by the balls. I'm so out of my element I barely recognize myself. If any other woman on earth stepped into my line of sight with this much obvious innocence, I wouldn't even glance at them. What is it about this one?

I lean back and cross one leg over the other, trying to appear far more relaxed than I feel. It's not that I lack confidence. It's that I want to grab her, arrange her straddling my lap, and kiss her senseless while she rubs her pussy against my cock until she comes in her jeans.

I don't think Faye would appreciate that.

"What's in the bag?" I tease, nodding toward where I dropped our purchases from the fetish shop over by the door.

She shakes her head and giggles. "You'll have to wait and see."

"How long will I have to wait?"

She shrugs. "I don't know."

"Is it something you can comfortably wear on the second floor in front of other people tonight?"

She shrugs again. "I don't think Barbara had anything in stock I could comfortably wear even in private, but I'm going to do it anyway. It will be out of my comfort zone, but it covers all the important stuff. Plus, I've been out of my comfort zone from the moment I stepped into Edge for your class two weeks ago."

I smile. "You seem more relaxed with me after spending the day with me."

"I am." And yet, she's sitting rigidly on the edge of the cushion, spine straight, hands rubbing her thighs. She looks like she's about to have a tooth extracted, but it's an improvement over looking like she's about to have *all* her teeth removed.

I'm going to get right to the point. "Asher said he thought you would enjoy being exposed to other people."

She swallows. "He said that to me, too. I had trouble sleeping last night because I couldn't get his words out of my head."

"And here I thought you had trouble sleeping because you were nervous about our date this morning."

"That, too."

"I only watched you observe one scene, but if you reacted to all of the scenes that way, he might be right. What comes to mind when you think of other people seeing you naked?"

"It's the craziest notion. The only person who isn't a doctor who has ever seen any part of me naked is Barbara a few hours ago."

My cock stiffens at the reminder. "And yet, the idea is titillating."

She licks those pretty lips. I love it when she does

that. "I don't know. I think it's maybe in combination with the submission. It's not that I want to take my clothes off while people watch, it's that..." She chews on her lip, thinking or unwilling to continue because the next words freak her out.

I fill in the blank for her. "It's the idea of being forced to do so. Having a Dom order you to strip or taking away your ability to protest because you're hands aren't even free."

She shudders and looks away.

I uncross my leg and drop it to the floor before leaning forward. "Look at me, baby."

She shifts her gaze to mine, her bottom lip trapped between her teeth.

"It's not uncommon. There's no reason to be embarrassed. Lots of people like to be dominated in that way."

"I'm not lots of people," she murmurs.

*You certainly are not.* "You're human. Most people would find themselves somewhere on the kink spectrum if they would loosen up, educate themselves, and open their minds. It's invigorating imagining yourself letting me be in control."

"What if I see one of the members at my grocery store or, God forbid, my office? I would die."

"What happens inside a kink club stays inside a kink club. It's a cardinal rule. If you see someone you know from Edge out in vanilla society, you walk right on by and pretend you don't know them. They will, too. It's common courtesy. If you want to discuss it with them later, do so when you see them again here. Establish a firm boundary."

"I don't know if I'm ready for people to see me naked. It's so farfetched I can't believe we're discussing it."

"Then we won't take that step tonight. It's off the table. How about if you put that outfit on, and we'll do a practice scene right here." I nod toward the bench in the middle of the room.

She glances toward the corners of the room. "Are there cameras?"

"No. There are no cameras on this floor, nor in any of the private rooms on the second floor, the bathrooms, or the locker rooms—just the main play area."

"Are you going to strap me down?" she asks, her voice shaking.

"If that's what you want. We're negotiating every detail now. There will be no surprises when we start the scene."

"It seems like it would be boring if I knew everything you were going to do."

I chuckle. "In the future, not anytime soon, mind you, but when you're more established, *that* can be something we negotiate—whether you want me to surprise you or shock you. I can't know what would cross the line for you yet, and neither can you."

She nods. "So I change into that outfit, and then what?"

"Then we take things slow. I'll restrain you and see how you feel. I'll bare your bottom and see how you feel. I'll swat you and check in again. One step at a time. You have to communicate with me, and you have to be truthful always. If I ever find out you lied to me or said what you thought I wanted to hear, I will discipline you in a way you will not enjoy."

She flinches. "What way is that?"

"Orgasm denial is always an excellent punishment."

Her eyes go wide. "I don't understand."

"You will if you lie to me." I lift a brow.

She shivers. It's so fucking sexy.

"Are you ready?"

"I guess."

I rise and head for the door to grab the bag. When I return, before handing it to her, I say, "You need a safe-word. Have you thought about one?"

"Liver." She makes a gagging face.

I smile. "I take it you don't like liver."

"It's gross."

"You thought this through, didn't you?"

"Yes. I think everything through," she admits proudly.

I'm sure she does. I've seen evidence of it many times today. She wouldn't be here with me now if she hadn't already decided she would accept this invitation long before I offered.

I like knowing she thought about me dominating her and was hoping I would ask. "Go change, baby." I hand her the bag and point toward the bathroom.

She stands, but she looks more pale than usual as she takes the shopping bag from me and heads for the bathroom.

I drop back onto the loveseat and run my hands through my hair. I can't believe I've spent the day with Faye. It's even harder to believe we've ended up here in my club, and she's about to submit to me.

I stare at the bathroom door. I'm certain she will be a while. She likes to think things through. If she's not feeling it, she will come back out in her street clothes. And I have to be okay with that.

What if she can't let herself relax and submit to me? Dominating her is my life force now. On the other hand, we had an amazing day together, and I only dominated her in subtle ways. I didn't want to scare her.

All I could think about was the fact that no one has touched her. I'm the first man to kiss her. That should freak me the fuck out, but it doesn't. It makes me want to wrap her up, take her home, and make her mine in every imaginable way.

I have to make sure my head is on straight. I'm not in the habit of training a submissive. I need to take things slowly and watch closely for signs of distress.

I pull out my phone and shoot off a quick text to Drake, letting him know I'm on the third floor with Faye and that I'm not certain when we will be done.

His response is quick—a thumbs-up emoji and then a laughing emoji. He's going to say, "I told you so," for the next ten years, and I'm oddly okay with that.

When the bathroom door opens, I snap my attention in that direction. Faye steps into the room, and I stop breathing.

She's wearing a slinky black negligée. I can tell from here that the material drapes around her body perfectly. Her full pert breasts are hugged by two triangles that cover them demurely while leaving nothing to the imagination. Tiny, delicate spaghetti straps hold the lingerie in place. A lace edge runs down her cleavage. The material gathers under her breasts, leaving the rest of the silk to fall down loosely below her bottom. The same lace that's between her breasts edges the bottom hem.

Faye has pulled her hair up. She had a clip in it all day, but she has gathered most of it in that clip now so that it hangs in long ringlets down her back. I love that she's barefoot. I know she isn't a fan of heels. I don't care that much about heels. I'd rather my submissive be comfortable.

"Come here, baby." My voice is off. It's low and cracks with every word.

She shuffles toward me.

"You're stunning, Faye. You take my breath away."

Her cheeks are pink, and she's biting the corner of her lower lip in that way that makes my cock harder than a rock.

"Turn around, baby."

She spins away from me, letting me see her backside. Fuck she's spectacular. Every inch of her. Her skin is creamy white with a smattering of freckles. This is the first time I'm seeing her thighs, and I desperately want to spread them and lick a line up to her pussy.

"You have no idea how gorgeous you are, Faye. Turn back around, baby."

Her hands are fisted at her sides. I'm sure she doesn't know what to do with them.

I grab two pillows from the loveseat and drop them next to each other on the floor in front of me. "Kneel for me, Faye. One knee in the center of each pillow."

I watch her closer than I've ever watched another sub in my life. I want to be absolutely certain I don't push her to do something that doesn't turn her on.

She awkwardly kneels before me just as I instructed, which leaves her knees parted wide.

"Good girl. You can sit back on your heels if it's more comfortable for you."

I wait for her to try that position, relieved when she draws in a deep breath. Her gaze is lowered. She probably learned to look down in a video, but I want her to look up. I want to see her eyes.

I've situated her close enough that I can lean my elbows on my knees and reach out and touch her if I want. I don't touch her yet. I thread my fingers together between my knees. "Clasp your hands behind your back, Faye, and lift your head. I want your eyes."

She does as she's told. She's trembling, but I'm confident she's pleased with her reaction so far.

"Good girl." I reach out and gently stroke her cheek, nearly coming in my jeans when she tips her head toward my hand.

I'm still wearing what I wore all day. In a minute, I will change so that she sees me in a different role.

"How do you feel, Faye?"

She swallows. "Good."

"When we're playing, I want you to call me Sir."

Her pretty cheeks pinken.

"Try it. How do you feel, baby?"

"Fine, Sir." She shivers.

I want to look down at the rest of her body, but I hold her gaze instead. I'll get a better look at the rest of her soon. "What are you wearing under the negligée, Faye?"

"A G-string, Sir."

"Do you like it?"

She scrunches up her nose. "I'm not sure yet, Sir. I've never worn one before. It's strange having a strap between my cheeks. Feels weird."

"Sometimes, I'll want you to wear something over your pussy. If you don't like the G-string, I'll buy you some other panties that are more comfortable, okay?"

"Yes, Sir."

"I'm going to go change now. I want you to stay in this position while I'm gone. Think about your submission and how it makes you feel."

"Yes, Sir."

When I rise, I lean over and kiss her forehead. "Good girl."

# CHAPTER 10

FAYE

My head is spinning. Twelve hours ago, I was trying to decide what to wear to have coffee with Easton. Now, I'm kneeling in his private playroom in his private club wearing the most provocative outfit I've ever worn in my life.

I should be scandalized, and in a way, I am. But I'm aroused, too. Something snapped inside me when I kneeled in front of him. I like it. I don't care right now that maybe it's incredibly kinky and most of society would be appalled. I only care how I feel, and I like it.

If this were any other man, I would probably be unable to trust so easily, but this is Easton. I didn't know him well in high school. How could I have? I was a freshman. He was a senior. I barely knew him. I only spoke to him in passing. But somehow, it's enough for me to feel like he wouldn't dare take advantage of me or do anything to hurt me.

Besides, he has an impeccable reputation with the community. This club has mostly five-star ratings. I did a search. Since it's a discreet private club, there isn't much to find, but I found enough chatter to know it's extremely reputable.

I don't wait long. I'm sure Easton didn't want to leave me with my thoughts longer than necessary. He's probably worried I will jump up and run from the building. However, I couldn't have done that while he was in the bathroom since my street clothes were in there with him.

He's back. I can feel his presence behind me. It's powerful. He's so very Dominant. His power over me is thick in the room.

"Rise, baby."

I release my hands and awkwardly come to my feet. It's not graceful, but he doesn't comment.

"Come here." He takes one of my hands as I turn toward him. He takes my breath away. He's wearing black slacks and a black button-down with the sleeves rolled up to his elbows. He has on black loafers, and he exudes sex appeal.

Easton guides me across the room to a wall I haven't paid attention to. I noticed the bench and a padded table in the middle of the room, but now, I see there is a lot of fetish equipment on the walls.

He leads me to a pegboard. "Stand against the board facing the room, Faye."

I do as I'm told. My breathing is heavy from anticipation and nerves.

He lifts my chin and meets my gaze. "You have my word I will never do anything that will injure you physically or emotionally. I will never strike your skin harder than what it takes to leave you pink for a few hours. I will never do anything without explaining myself."

"Yes, Sir," I whisper. I like calling him *Sir*. It makes me tingle all over. I also like this scrap of material I'm wearing because he's looking at me like he wants to eat me alive. For the first time in my life, I feel sexy. I want to bottle up this feeling and recreate it over and over.

For the first time in my life, I feel like I can trust someone. He's not going to run to his brother and friends after this and laugh about my inexperience or how awkward I am. Is he?

He frowns. "What just went through your mind, baby. Don't overthink. Just tell me."

I swallow. "Are you going to tell anyone about this?"

His brows rise. "If you mean the specifics of what we do behind closed doors, never. My brother knows we're in my apartment, though. I texted him so he would know why I won't be in my office soon."

I lick my lips. "You won't tell him what we do." I need to be sure.

"No, Faye. What we do alone is private, especially since you've made it clear that you want it that way. I'm close to my brother and several friends I've had for years, but I never talk about my sex life with them. This isn't high school. We don't high five and laugh about our conquests from the night before."

I gasp. He has no idea how close to home that hits. That's exactly my concern. "Did you do that in high school?" For some reason the idea bothers me.

He shakes his head. "No." A slow smile grows on his face. "I didn't have sex with girls in high school, Faye. Do you not remember how dorky I was?"

I return the smile. My body warms. He's said everything just right. I feel better, and I'm glad I spoke my mind. "I was far dorkier," I say, lightening the mood.

He chuckles. "You'll never win in a dork-meter contest with me, baby. But I can tell you that you're certainly not dorky now." He sets a finger on my chest and grazes it down between my cleavage.

"Neither are you." My heart is racing. I don't think he meant for us to have a conversation while we're about to do whatever it is we're about to do, but I like that he doesn't seem to mind. He's the one who encouraged me to speak my mind.

Easton eases his hand up and grips my chin before leaning in to kiss my neck.

I shiver. His touch does that to me.

His voice is deep and low when he speaks. "I want you to spread your legs wide so I can put a spreader bar between your ankles. Have you seen a spreader bar before, baby?"

I shiver again as I nod, partly because I have seen the device he's talking about, both in the club last night and online. However, the main reason I'm trembling is because I love it when he calls me *baby*. It makes me feel special. Cherished.

"After I secure your ankles, I'm going to lift your arms over your head and attach them to the pegboard. Are you okay with that?"

I nod.

"Words, baby."

"I'm okay with that, Sir."

"Good girl."

His praise is even better than his endearment. I want to be his *baby* and his *good girl*. It sends a chill down my spine.

When he squats down in front of me, I grab his shoulders to steady myself while he nudges my feet as wide as he wants them.

I flinch at the sound of the bar tapping the floor between my feet, and I hold my breath while he cuffs my ankles in soft leather.

As he rises, he smooths his palms up my legs. "How does that make you feel, baby?" His voice is gentle and caring.

"Vulnerable."

He smiles. "That's the goal. Is your pussy wet?"

My face heats.

He takes my chin again and leans closer. "Is your pussy wet, Faye?"

"Yes, Sir," I breathe.

"Good girl. Lift your arms over your head for me."

I'm shaking as I obey him, and everything changes. I'm stretched out so far that my breasts are high and the hem of my negligée is no longer concealing anything. I don't have to look down to know. I lifted my arms while I was still in the bathroom to find out what would happen.

I catch a glimpse of two large metal circles before Easton pushes them into the pegboard higher than I can reach. He cuffs my wrists next, and when I tip my head back, I see that I'm attached to the eye bolts.

He steps back a few inches and lets his gaze roam up and down my body. "You're so damn sexy, Faye." His voice is reverent.

I feel as sexy as he insists I am. "Thank you, Sir."

"How do you feel now, baby?" He takes another step back.

"Significantly more vulnerable, Sir."

"Good. I like how the hem of your negligée is high enough for me to see your thong. Your pussy is shaved."

I swallow and nod. "I've shaved it for years. I don't like the feel of the hair. Is that okay?" I assume he won't mind. Nearly all of the women I saw in the club last night were shaved bare.

"Of course. I'm just surprised is all. I like it, though. I can't wait to run my cheek against your pussy."

I whimper.

He smiles. "You like that thought."

"Yes, Sir."

"Your breasts are spectacular, Faye. I'm dying to see them fully, but I love how high they rise on your chest with your arms above your head."

I involuntarily arch my chest toward him. I feel greedy. For the first time in my life, I desperately want someone to touch them. I want *Easton* to touch them. They feel heavy. My nipples are hard. He can see them pressing against the thin silk.

"Mmm. I love seeing you arch your needy breasts toward me. Do you want me to stroke them, Faye?"

"Yes, please, Sir."

"Such good manners for a new submissive. I'll reward you for that." He steps closer and slowly trails one finger up the center of my body between my breasts.

I'm so eager for him to touch my nipples that I lean into his touch.

"Stay still, baby. I'll touch you when I'm ready. You won't control the narrative."

A whimper escapes my lips. It's hard to remain still. Even though I'm stretched out, I can still sway back and forth a few inches.

I lower my gaze and watch as he trails one finger

around my breast in a slow, excruciating spiral. When he gets close to my nipple, I hold my breath, anticipating how good it will feel for him to touch it, but then he stops and switches to the other breast.

I give a frustrated moan.

He smiles, removes his hand from my breast entirely, and lifts my chin with one finger. "Who decides when you get pleasure, Faye?"

I can hardly breathe. "You do, Sir."

"Part of submitting to me includes patience. Your arousal will heighten from your submission. I want to give you pleasure. You'll earn it if you stand very still for me."

I nod erratically and glance toward the bench in the middle of the room. "I thought you were going to spank me, Sir."

"Oh, I definitely am. We'll get to that. I think you need a more sensual experience first. Don't you?"

"Yes, Sir." It's the only answer. I didn't watch any scenes like this downstairs last night. There were certainly sensual aspects of every scene, but I didn't see any of the Doms restrain the subs and then torment them with nothing but teasing touches.

He reaches toward my wrist, drags his finger down my arm, skips my armpit, and continues toward my breast.

My vision blurs. I've never imagined anything like this in my life. I can't believe how aroused I am. The only times I'm ever aroused are when I'm alone under my covers at night, touching myself with my vibrator.

Until Easton. He arouses me when he steps into a room. It's frightening because I want this so badly while, at the same time, I know I'm inevitably going to get hurt. I'm growing surer of that fact by the hour.

He's intrigued by me. I'm a plaything. A challenge.

He finds me attractive, and he wants to be the one to show me all about BDSM. It can't last. How long will he be interested in me and keep me around before he grows bored?

I shake my concerns from my head because I'm here now, and I want this. I will deal with the fallout later. This isn't me. I can't sustain this alternate Faye forever. Eventually, I'll go back to my real life...my boring existence as a scientist, my vanilla world where everything is orderly and precise.

I arch again when Easton circles my other nipple. I can't control my body. I want him to touch me so badly. Maybe I'm making a horrible decision giving my submission and my body to this man, but I'm going to do it anyway and deal with the consequences later. Maybe I can guard my heart.

My heart is not something I ever imagined needing to guard. Until Easton, I've never been in a single situation where I thought myself capable of craving carnal pleasure or the company of another person in my life. I figured I was broken.

If I'm not broken, and I just hadn't met the right person to tap into my inner kinky self, then I'm in deep trouble when this ends.

*Stop worrying about tomorrow.*

"Get out of your head and look at me, Faye," he orders.

I meet his gaze. It's intense. Brows furrowed. He's commanding me with his look. He doesn't glance away as his finger reaches down behind my knee and trails up the back of my thigh.

The ridiculous triangle between my legs is soaked, and a new rush of wetness leaks out of me. I'm certain he will eventually touch it, which embarrasses me. Should I be this wet?

He eases his finger under the back of my negligee and up my butt cheek until he reaches the strap holding up my G-string. Tucking his finger under the elastic, he gives it a slight tug, causing it to pull tighter between my cheeks.

It's an unusual sensation because I've never worn anything this skimpy before. I never thought I would like it, and I didn't when I first put it on, but now that I'm at Easton's mercy, I kind of like that he has access to my skin. It feels naughty and sexy.

He holds my gaze as his finger trails down the strap between my cheeks until I rise onto my toes and clench my butt when he gets too close to my forbidden hole.

"Easton..."

"One day, you will let me touch you here without clenching."

My face heats.

"Eventually, you will trust me to take care of you and know your limits."

My lips tremble. The thought of him touching my tight, forbidden hole is so foreign I can't wrap my head around it. Luckily, he moves on, dragging his finger back up the strap and around to my belly button.

"Where do you need my touch, baby?" he asks in a sultry voice. "Your pussy or your nipples?"

I moan. "Both, Sir."

"Mmm. Do you think you've earned my touch?"

"Yes, Sir." I can't think that I've done anything to warrant denial.

Suddenly, both his hands are on my hips under my

negligée. His thumbs graze my belly. "Do you want me to see your breasts, Faye?"

"Yes, Sir." God, I want that so much. I want to see him looking at me. I want to see the lust in his eyes. I want to feel sexy, and I know I will. I already feel sexier than I've ever felt, but I know it will grow tenfold when he sees me naked.

He removes his hands from my hips, pulls them out from under the silk, and wraps them around my torso just below my breasts. His thumbs reach higher now, tormenting the undersides of my breasts. It's maddening and driving me wild.

"Your nipples are so hard, baby. Achingly hard. I like seeing them through the cups of your negligée."

"They hurt, Sir," I murmur because it's true.

Finally, he flicks them both over the silk with his thumbs.

I cry out as though he has thrust into my channel.

"Fuck, you're responsive. It makes my cock harder than it's ever been. You have no idea what you do to me."

"Show me," I blurt out boldly, surprised by my request.

He shakes his head. "Not tonight, baby. Tonight is about you."

He's seriously not going to let me see him tonight?

He brings his hands to the V of my negligée, trails his fingers down the lace, and eases the cups lower until my nipples are free.

I arch and moan as the cool air in the room touches my aching tips.

"Spectacular, Faye," he whispers reverently. "You're divine. I could play with these little berries all night. I bet I could make you come from nipple stimulation alone. I want to suckle them and circle them with my tongue. I want to make you writhe with need."

"Please..."

"Patience, baby. You'll take what I offer when I offer it."

"Yes, Sir." Blood is pumping through my body. I'm on fire. His words drive me crazier than his fingers. I want more. I want everything. I wish he hadn't declared that he would not have sex with me tonight. I want him inside me.

I crave this unknown like a drug. It's elusive, but I want it. I've never once in my life wanted to have sex with someone, but suddenly, I'm salivating for it.

Easton releases the cups, and they return to their original position, covering me.

I whimper.

A moment later, he grabs the hem at my hips and lifts the entire garment up my body so fast I'm stunned. He raises it up my arms until he reaches my hands. "Open your fists, Faye."

When I obey him, he tucks the silk into my hands. "Hold this up for me. If you release it, I will punish you."

A deep shudder courses through my body at his words. Does he know how it affects me when he talks like that? Of course, he does. He's a Dom. He owns this club. He's a very talented Dom who's playing my body mercilessly.

I grip the silk as he steps back. He doesn't hide his obvious perusal of my body. I'm stretched out in front of him, my breasts high and heavy. The only thing covering me is the triangle of black material over my pussy.

I've never been exposed like this. It's so naughty. It's

heady, and my arousal is growing by the second as he stares at me.

"You are perfection, Faye. Every inch of you. I'm going to enjoy looking at you often. You like it. I'll keep you naked often when we're together. I'll put you on display for my pleasure in obscene positions. You'll obey my requests because it feels so good when I look at you."

I swallow. My throat is dry.

"You like it when I look at you, don't you, baby?"

"Yes, Sir," I whisper.

"You've thought a lot about what it would feel like to be exposed like this, haven't you, Faye?"

"Yes, Sir."

"It won't be enough. Soon, you'll want me to let other people look at you, too."

My breath hitches. I know he's right, but it's embarrassing.

"I won't share you yet. Not tonight. Another night. I'll strap your naked body spread wide on a St. Andrew's cross on the second floor and use a feather to keep your nipples hard while people watch."

I moan. My nipples tighten further.

"Just so we're clear, while you're under my tutelage, I will not let anyone else touch you. You will submit to me and me alone. I will choose when and how to expose you. You will obey my wishes. Understood?"

"Yes, Sir." My mouth is so dry I'm panting. His words have so much power.

"Do you want me to expose your pussy, Faye?"

I nod. "Please, Sir." I'm wanton and greedy. I'm someone else—a parallel Faye. I don't know her, and I don't care. I'm in heaven.

I wonder how he will expose me with my legs spread so wide.

He steps toward a tall dresser a few feet to my side, opens the top drawer, and returns with a pair of scissors. My breath hitches. The blades put a certain amount of fear in me. In seconds, he snips one side of my thong, letting it fall to the floor around my ankle.

It's shocking. Unexpected. Hotter than hell.

I don't have time to ponder it further before Easton squats in front of me, grips my thighs, and stares at my pussy. He inhales deeply and groans. "Fuck, you smell good."

I shiver. His breath is driving me mad, and I tip my head back and moan loudly when he rubs his nose against my mons. It's so dirty. So naughty. So sexy.

He abandons my pussy, rising to stand in front of me again. I'm disappointed, but it's short-lived because before I know it, he flicks his tongue over my nipple.

I cry out.

He blows on the wet tip. "The prettiest ripe berries ever. So pink and swollen and needy. These nipples will look amazing when I clamp them and let a chain hang between them.

I writhe. I can't help it. His dirty talk drives me out of my mind. Will he really clamp my tender flesh? I've read about it. I've seen sketches online. I can't imagine it, though. However, I don't think he tosses out idle threats. I trust he will eventually do everything he has suggested.

"You like that idea, don't you, Faye?"

I whimper.

"Words, baby. Do you want me to clamp these tender buds?"

I nod. "Yes, Sir."

"Mmm. Someday," he teases.

# CHAPTER 11

EASTON

Christ, she's incredible. I've dominated a lot of women, and none of them compare to this experience. Faye is so pure.

I keep surprising myself with my ability to bring her to the dark side. I haven't worked with a newbie in so long that I don't remember it.

This isn't some random woman asking me to train her. She didn't ask me to train her at all. I took this on myself. I hardly gave her an option. The thought of letting someone else work with her still makes me cringe. It's not going to happen.

When I decided to bring her to the club before it opened, I hadn't intended to lead her straight to my third-floor play space and keep her all to myself. It just happened, and I'm not sorry. I really do not feel like sharing her.

I love that I'm standing before her naked body, and no

BECCA JAMESON

one else can see it. I love that she's so fucking hot for me she can't stand still. Her nipples are perfection. Her pussy is dripping. The fact that she shaves nearly brought me to my knees when I first saw her bare pussy.

I will expose her on the second floor another night. I think she needs the experience. I'm not such a greedy bastard that I would deny her something she craves. But for tonight, I want her to myself. I want several of her firsts to be mine alone.

I'm taking my sweet time because it's so delicious watching her squirm and nearly beg. Her ripe body is desperate. She's struggling to focus.

I reach for the nipples I've been admiring and pinch them.

She rises onto her toes again, which is difficult with her feet spread wide. "Ohh…"

I pinch harder and twist, watching her closely to see if she likes the bite of pain. Some women do not. Faye's eyes roll back, though. She loves it.

"Please…"

Damn, I love that word coming from her lips. I love how she keeps licking them, unable to keep them damp. I will give her water as soon as I make her come. I release her nipples and lean in close so I'm breathing in her ear. "You'll come when I tell you to, baby. Not before."

I don't want to set her up for failure. There are few women I've met in my life who could come on command, and I have no idea if Faye might ultimately be one of them, but what I do know is she's very close to orgasm, and I will be able to recognize when she is on the edge. That's when I'll demand she peak for me…when it's inevitable.

116

"Yes, Sir," she breathes. I adore the shiver that wracks her body yet again.

"I need to taste you, baby. Are you ready for that? Are you ready to have my mouth on your pussy?"

"Yes, Sir..."

I drop to my knees, grab her thighs, and bring my mouth to her dripping pussy. The first lick makes me moan. She tastes like heaven. She's addictive. I'm going to want more. I will wake up tomorrow craving her on my lips.

When I suck her pussy into my mouth, she cries out. *"Easton..."*

I love my name on her lips. She knows exactly who is dominating her. She's with me and only me.

She's far too close to leave her hanging any longer, so I thrust my tongue into her tight cunt and then trap her clit with my teeth while I flick it.

Her breath hitches. She stops breathing. She's on the edge.

I release her, press my thumb firmly against her clit, and order, "Come, Faye."

She shakes violently as her orgasm washes over her. Her entire body is involved. And she screams. I love how uninhibited she is. She has no idea she's screaming. I need to remember that. If she screamed like that in the main room downstairs, she would interrupt everyone else's scene.

I ease my thumb off her clit only when she starts panting and struggles to hold herself up.

Instantly, I rise, wrap an arm around her middle, and reach up to detach her wrists from the pegs. Two quick jerks on the Velcro, and she collapses against me.

I brace her with my hands on her torso. "Can you hold on to me while I release your ankles, baby?"

She nods and grabs my shoulders as I squat before her.

I'm quick and have her cradled in my arms in seconds. She brings me to my knees. I didn't start this day picturing holding her naked body twelve hours later.

I grab a bottle of water from my minifridge, take a seat on the loveseat, and keep her tucked against me.

She pulls her arms in close to her chest and snuggles into my embrace.

I twist off the lid of the water and bring it to her lips. "You need to drink, baby."

She shakes her head. "Not thirsty."

I chuckle and use one finger to lift her chin so she has to look at me. "Did I ask if you were thirsty?"

Her eyes go wide. "No, Sir."

"Trust me. You're thirsty. It's important to drink plenty of fluids after an intense scene. I'd still like to lower you onto that bench and spank your bottom if you're up to it in a few minutes. Do you want that to be for fun or for punishment?" I lift a brow.

She gasps, sits up straighter on my lap, and opens her mouth to accept the water when I hold it to her lips once again.

"Good girl."

She downs nearly all of it. "You were right."

I grin. "I'm often right. I'm a Dom, after all."

She leans back in my arms and stares at me. "I should be embarrassed."

I cock my head to one side. "Why?"

She brings her arms in to cover her breasts. "I'm naked. You're not. And you just…"

"Ate your pretty cunt?" I supply.

She rolls her eyes. "Yeah, that."

I reach for one of her wrists and lower her arm. "Don't cover yourself, baby. I like looking at you, plus I think you crave the embarrassment. It's part of your need to be exposed. You want me to look at you. You want me to expose you."

She bites her lip. I know I'm right, but I know it's hard for her to admit. "No one has ever made me feel like you do before," she whispers.

I smile. "Sexy?"

"Yes."

"You are so unbelievably sexy. I'm sorry no one else has ever made you feel that truth, but I suspect it's not because no one saw you that way. I bet you didn't notice they were looking."

She slowly nods. "Maybe."

"Are you worn out? Or do you want to try my bench?" I wiggle my brows.

She turns to look at the apparatus in the center of the room. "I want to try it, Sir."

That one word does cruel things to my cock. If she notices it pressing against her, she isn't giving me any indication.

I rise, still holding her, and carry her to my spanking bench. It's my favorite piece of equipment. I had it specially made. It's one of a kind.

I lower Faye to her feet at the end of the bench and pull a hair scrunchie out of my pocket. When she glances to see me holding it between my lips while I remove the clip and gather her curls up on top of her head, she giggles. "Did you pull that out of thin air?"

After plucking it from my mouth to secure her hair, I

chuckle. "A prepared Dom always has a hair tie in their pocket." I grab her hips and lift her. "Knees on the padded section below the bench."

She's trembling. I love it.

"Lean over the bench so your breasts hang between the two sections. Your face lines up with the hole in the third section."

The reason I love this bench is because it doesn't leave a woman's breasts flattened on the bench. It has an opening where they can hang below. The hole for her face keeps her from having to turn her head one way or the other.

"Good girl. Put your forearms on the other padded sections."

Her breaths deepen as she settles into position. She's like a piece of art. I want to worship her. I'm going to.

I adjust the armrests slightly, and then I move the kneepads wider and slightly closer to her arms.

She shudders violently. She's so exposed. I doubt she even realizes how fully on display she is with her pussy open like this. I can see her rosebud, too. Pink and tight and waiting for me to train it.

"I'm going to restrain you now. Remember your safeword."

"Yes, Sir."

I have an extensive restraint system on this bench, and I watch her closely as I move around. First, I secure her wrists, then her ankles. I pull a thick strap across the center of her back and then the back of her head.

She moans when I secure her head. Her body stiffens, and she lifts her hips off the bench. It's the only part of her not secured, but since she has tested me, I add yet another strap across her hips.

Now, her breathing is wild and erratic. She tugs and squirms.

I set a hand on the small of her back. "Relax your body, baby. Don't fight it. The restraints help you submit deeper. Give yourself to me."

"I'm nervous," she whispers.

"I know you are, baby, but I will never do anything to hurt you. Do you know why I've restrained you so totally?"

"Why?"

"Because every additional strap drove your arousal higher."

"You can't know that."

I chuckled. "I know everything. I know by the way you breathe, the color of your skin, and how you tense. I know by the soft moans you make, the smell of your pussy, and the arousal leaking out. You're so horny you're going to drip on the floor."

She moans deeply.

"It feels good to turn your power over to me. It feels good to submit."

She whimpers.

I slide my hand down to her fantastic ass. "This is the prettiest bottom I've ever seen." I move around to stand between her spread legs and palm both globes at once. I pull them apart, making her squeak.

"Easton..."

"I won't penetrate your bottom tonight, Faye. You're not ready for that. I haven't even been inside your cunt except with my tongue. But mark my words, one day I will push my finger into your tight bottom and make you come so hard you scream."

She clenches her cheeks as she moans. She's so turned

on, and my cock keeps getting harder and harder as she responds to me so delightfully.

I slide my hands down to her thighs and pull her labia apart. I know the cool air in the room will hit her wet folds and drive her crazy.

She tries to lift her head and groans when she comes up short. Her panting is heavy. "Oh, God..."

I haven't done anything yet. My girl is so submissive that she's close to orgasm from the restraints and the fact that she's starting to realize the control I have over her body now that she can't move.

"Your pussy needs more attention, doesn't it, baby?"

"Yes, Sir. Please..."

"How many orgasms can you have in one evening?"

"I don't know. I've only ever had one."

I adjust my cock. *Fuck me.*

After releasing her perfect globes, I move to her side and reach under to fondle a loose breast.

Faye squirms as much as she can. "Sir..."

"It's powerful, isn't it? Submitting to me. Knowing I can touch you whenever and wherever I want. Knowing I decide when to stroke your skin or leave you wanting. Knowing that, at any moment, I'm going to spank your perfect bottom hard enough to send vibrations to your pussy and drive you mad with need."

The next sound she makes is unintelligible. And so sexy.

I tweak her nipple. "These rosy buds are so gorgeous, all swollen and tight."

When I release it, she whimpers again.

"Are you ready for my palm on your bottom, Faye?"

"Yes, Sir."

"Safeword?"

"Liver, Sir."

"Good girl."

I don't need to steady her, but I set a palm on the small of her back anyway and rub her bottom with my other hand. I land the first swat on one cheek, making her gasp and flinch. Without much hesitation, I spank her other globe.

She flinches again, but not as forcefully.

I spank all around her pretty globes and the backs of her thighs with about a quarter of the intensity I would normally use on a seasoned submissive.

When I pause, I slide my hand into her messy bun and lean toward her ear. "How are you feeling, baby?"

"Mmm."

Oh yeah. She's in subspace. I knew it was possible from how strongly she reacted to our previous scene at the peg board. All I did over there was lightly touch her before sucking her off, and she practically left the stratosphere.

This is more intense. She's more restrained, and I've added impact play.

"Do you want more, Faye?"

"Mmmhmm..."

I smile. "Words, baby. Ask for what you want."

"Please spank me harder, Sir."

"Good girl." I return to her hip and lean over her leg to see her pussy. Soaked. Her folds are swollen and red. I can't wait to make her come. But not before I spank her some more and drive her need higher.

I've never felt this Dominant over another woman. She has given me more power than any submissive I've ever commanded. She doesn't even fully realize that. She can't. She's too new to the lifestyle. She can't grasp the nuances of submission.

I spank her harder, enjoying the way her bottom grows redder. Her skin is pale, so it pinkens easily. It's gorgeous. I want to rub my cheek against her warm skin. I will in time.

I listen closely to the noises she makes, picking up on her arousal as it intensifies until she emits a long, low groan that fills the room. Her body shakes violently with need. She's on the edge.

I immediately reach between her legs and thrust two fingers into her cunt. Fuck, she's tight.

Faye screams. Her channel grips my fingers hard over and over as waves of her release crash through her. Copious amounts of her arousal run down my hand. It's the sexiest thing I've ever witnessed, and I've been a Dom for a long time.

I'm in so much trouble.

# CHAPTER 12

FAYE

It takes me a long time to recover from what happened on that bench. I'm embarrassed even though Easton tells me over and over that my reaction is normal.

He unfastened me in seconds, wrapped me in a soft blanket, and has been holding me in his lap for an hour. He feeds me little bites of chocolate and makes me drink more water every few minutes.

He rubs my back. "It's called subspace, baby. It can be powerful. You'll probably feel hungover tomorrow, like you had too much to drink."

"I've never been hungover," I mumble.

"No? You've never overindulged in wine or cocktails and had a killer headache the next day?" He leans me back to look into my eyes.

He does this a lot. It's unnerving when he forces me to look at him. "I've never had alcohol," I tell him.

His brows lift. "You constantly surprise me."

"I'm weird. I told you that this morning."

"You're not weird, Faye. You're refreshing. I should feel bad for tempting you down this path into my kinky lair."

I roll my eyes. "I'm the one who came to your class and got intrigued. I don't think you get credit for luring me in."

"That may be, but I'm the one who told you to call and handed you my card. I'm the one who asked you to come back, invited you to brunch, and then took over your life today."

His smile makes me tremble. He says all these serious words while grinning at me. Sometimes, I have trouble reading him. However, I read him better than any other human I've ever met. Perhaps because he's blunt. He tells me what he's thinking. Heck, he also tells me what *I'm* thinking.

His phone vibrates in his pocket, making him wince. "That's my brother. He's texted several times. Do you mind if I check it?"

"No. Go ahead."

He leans to one side to pull it out of his pocket, taps the screen with one hand, and reads the messages. He somehow manages to return a text with just one thumb before stashing it and sighing.

"Everything okay?" I don't want to pry. "I'm keeping you from your club. I bet you're supposed to be working."

"Faye, you are not keeping me from anything. I'm right where I want to be. Drake has everything under control. He doesn't need me. He's only texting to harass me."

I frown. "Harass you?"

"Yep. I've told him repeatedly that I'm not ready for another relationship. I've insisted I don't train new submissives. Now he's going to laugh at me for months."

I stare at him. "Why?" This would be one of those times when I'm missing social cues.

He smiles and taps my nose. "Because he was right. You've lured me into your web, and now I'm trapped."

I frown. "You're trapped?" My brain is running slower than usual, probably because of the weird subspace he spoke of. I'm not following.

"Figure of speech, baby. Trapped in a good way. I just mean I feel drawn to you. I want to be the one to train you. I want to spend more time with you. Drake encouraged me to ask you out, and he was right. Does that scare you?"

I don't know. I'm certainly scared for a whole host of reasons, but I can't verbalize them. I can't tell him how hard it is for me to trust or why I don't let people get close to me. It's confusing. My weird issues go all the way back to high school. I never got over the way other kids treated me. I never gave adults the chance to do the same thing.

He rolls me closer to his body, holding me tightly. He kisses the top of my head. "You're exhausted. I've monopolized your day and night. I should take you home and tuck you into bed."

He's confusing me. He wants me to go home? "Okay."

He leans me back and looks me in the eyes, brows furrowed. "Are you okay, Faye?"

I nod. "Yes, Sir."

He brings his mouth to mine and kisses me gently. When he releases my lips, he groans. "You're going to distract me day and night. I can't get enough of you."

I assume that's a good thing? I don't ask. I feel heavy and tired.

Easton holds me closer and stands. He carries me to the bathroom, sets me on my feet, and reaches for the pile of clothes I carefully set on the counter when I changed. He grabs my panties first, squats in front of me, and taps my ankle. "Hold my shoulders, baby. Let me dress you."

It's so weird standing here naked, letting this man I barely know dress me. Except, it doesn't seem like I hardly know him. It seems like I've known him for a very long time. It seems like today was a month long.

Before I know it, I'm fully dressed, and my sexy black negligée is back in its bag. The thong is history since Easton cut it. The memory of that moment will never leave me. It might be the single most sexy thing I've ever experienced.

"I don't have a car..." I mumble absently as he guides me to the door of his apartment.

He turns toward me and cups my face. "Faye, I'm going to take you home and tuck you into bed myself, baby. You're dazed from the scene."

"We didn't go to the club..."

He smiles. "Nope. You're in no state of mind for that now. We'll do that next time."

Next time... I'm not sure I can survive another day like today. I'm so far out of my element that I don't know who I am. I think I've taken leave of my senses, or perhaps someone else inhabited my body for the day against my will.

Easton opens the door and leads me back to his office.

Drake is there, and when he turns around, he smiles. "Hey, Faye. It's good to see you."

"You, too," I whisper. I don't know how to act. I feel

uncomfortable and nervous. Does he know what we just did? Even though Easton said he would not talk about what we do alone, I'm sure Drake can surmise.

Easton sets his hands on my shoulders. "I'm going to take Faye home. I'll be back in a while."

Drake nods. His brow is furrowed. "Stay as long as you need. She's in deep."

In deep? What does that mean?

"Yes, she is. She slides into subspace easily."

Oh, subspace... That must be what Drake is referring to. I still don't get it, but I will admit I feel strange. Is this what being drunk feels like?

"Sleep well, Faye," Drake says.

"Thank you."

Easton leads me down the stairs, stopping at the second floor. We step into the reception area. Marny is there.

"Marny, this is Faye," Easton says.

Marny smiles warmly. "I remember her from last night and the intro class."

"She's my guest. She has permission to go anywhere in the building."

Marny nods. "Got it."

"I'll be back in a while," Easton informs her before leading me out of the reception area and down the next flight of stairs. He stops again at the entrance to the club, where the huge man guards the door. I met him last night as well. Jax.

"Jax, this is Faye."

Jax may be a giant with an expression that's usually serious, but he also greets me warmly. "I remember."

"She can come and go as she pleases at any time," Easton informs him.

Jax nods. "I won't forget." He tips his head at me.

I feel like I'm spinning out of control. Everything seems confusing. Why is Easton making sure everyone knows who I am?

"Come," he whispers in my ear before he takes my hand and leads me to his car. He says nothing as he helps me into the front seat, buckles my belt, and rounds the car.

On the drive home, he holds my hand. When he pulls up to my apartment building and parks in the street, I stare at him. It takes me a moment to realize he knew where I lived from my paperwork.

He helps me out of the car and into the building, where he calls the elevator. "What floor, baby?" he asks when we step inside.

I giggle.

He chuckles. "What's funny?"

"I was wondering if you knew *everything* about me."

"I know your apartment number is four-twelve, but the number doesn't necessarily correlate with the fourth floor."

"It does this time."

He pushes the button for the fourth floor.

I'm not sure I could have done this on my own. I really feel confused. He seems undaunted by my weird state of mind. Instead of asking me for my keys, he takes my purse, opens it, and pulls them out. In seconds, he ushers me inside and straight through to my bedroom as if he knows the place.

It's not a stretch. There are two bedrooms, but they aren't hard to find. It's an apartment, not the governor's mansion.

He angles me toward the bathroom, sets my purse and

the bag with my negligée on the counter, and bends to remove my shoes. "Do you want to take a bath or shower tonight?"

I grab his shoulders as he pulls my jeans off my body. It's like I'm too slow to keep up with the pace. "Uh, no. I'll do it in the morning."

"Okay." He pulls my sweater off next and turns me toward the sink, where he puts toothpaste on my toothbrush and hands it to me. "Brush, baby."

I stare at it for a second, trying to remember what I'm meant to do. I sort of know this is a common task I do twice a day, but I'm not sure what it entails.

Easton crowds me from behind, takes the toothbrush from my hand, puts some water on it, and holds it to my mouth. "Open, baby," he says gently.

I do as I'm told and stare at him in the mirror as he brushes my teeth for me. My face heats. What's wrong with me? After he helps me rinse and spit, I look at him. "I feel drugged."

"It's the subspace, baby." He unfastens my bra next and then lowers my panties down my legs so that I'm once again naked in front of him. He's all business now, though. He's not gawking at me like he was earlier. He points toward the toilet. "Pee. I'll wait outside."

I watch as he leaves the bathroom and pulls the door almost shut.

I consider reaching out and closing it the rest of the way, but something stops me. He's so Dominant. If he'd wanted it shut, he would have shut it. So I turn toward the toilet and do my business, flushing and washing my hands after. I'm still rubbing the soap in when he pushes the door back open and joins me. He dries my hands and guides me toward my bed.

When we reach it, he pulls the covers back and pats the sheet. "Climb in."

"I need PJs."

He smiles. "You don't." He lifts me off my feet, deposits me on the mattress, and pulls the covers over me. He sits next to me and glances at my nightstand before setting his palm on the bed on the other side of my hips. "Good. You have water. Drink it if you wake up in the night. You're still going to feel sluggish in the morning. I want you to text me when you wake up."

He pops off the bed, heads for the bathroom, and returns with my phone, which he proceeds to plug into the charger on my nightstand before turning off the ringer.

He's so...controlling. It feels nice. It also feels scary.

"I need PJs," I say again, squirming against the sheets. I've never slept naked.

He chuckles. "You should get used to sleeping naked, Faye."

"Why?"

"Because that's how you'll sleep in my bed."

In his bed? My heart rate picks up. He intends for me to sleep in his bed...? "When?" I blurt that out before I can stop myself.

He leans over and kisses me gently. "When you're ready."

That makes no sense. "I don't, uh... I don't sleep in other people's beds," I tell him, though I sound like a teenager.

He chuckles again. "You're so fucking precious. I'm glad you haven't slept in anyone else's bed, but soon you will sleep with me, and it's not likely I will be able to let you go after you've been in my arms all night."

"In your arms?" I shake my head. There's no way I could sleep with someone touching me. Nor can I sleep naked.

"Definitely." He brushes a lock of hair from my face, reminding me it's still up in the bun he put it in. Everyone I saw as we left the club saw my disheveled hair. They must have thought we had sex.

Now, I'm mortified. I feel my face heat as I reach a hand up, touch my bun, and groan.

"What's wrong, Faye?"

"Everyone probably thinks we had sex," I hiss.

He doesn't laugh, but he looks like he's close. "Baby, it's none of their business if we had sex. It is, however, a fetish club. People have sex there. It's not permitted on the first floor, but the guests on the second and third floors often have sex. We even have showers in the locker room."

I groan and cover my face.

He strokes my arm. "I'm sorry you're embarrassed. I didn't mean to make you feel that way."

I drop my arm and glare at him. "You totally intend to embarrass me. You've said so."

He smiles. "In a scene. In the club. Yes. If that continues to be something you crave. But when we're not in a scene, and you're not specifically submitting to me, I never want you to be embarrassed."

I narrow my gaze. My brain is working better now. "I don't get the impression I would ever be not submitting to you."

He chuckles again. "Well, that's kind of true. It's hard for me to turn it off, especially when you enjoy it so much. I will, however, tone it down when we're not playing. I never want you to feel uncomfortable, baby."

I'm breathing heavily. My chest is rising and falling. He's hovering so close. Even lying here, he's dominating me. I'm pinned to my bed by his body on one side and his hand on the other. His gaze is so intense. Does he not realize that?

He lifts his hand and strokes my naked shoulder. "Will you sleep naked for me?"

I lick my lips. It's odd how he's asking so gently, but he's not really asking. He's inserting his will. "I'll try."

He glances at my nightstand. "Do you have a vibrator in there?"

My breath hitches, and my eyes go wide.

"Faye..." He's smirking now. "Is there a vibrator in your nightstand?"

"Yes, Sir," I murmur.

He opens it and takes it out. "Is this the only one you have?"

I nod slowly. What is he doing? I can't possibly have another orgasm tonight.

He shocks me speechless when he tucks it into his jacket pocket.

"What... What are you doing?" I ask.

He lifts my fingers to his lips and kisses them. "I don't want you to masturbate when I'm not with you."

I stop breathing.

He holds my gaze while he sucks the tip of my middle finger. "Don't use your fingers either. Don't touch your pussy."

Wetness rushes out of me. I'm going to get the sheets wet. Is he serious?

"You heard me. Your orgasms are mine."

My ears are ringing. I'm speechless. How can he

order me not to touch myself and be so blasé about it? Like it's a perfectly normal request.

He sets my hand down, stands, and leans over to kiss me again. I don't kiss him back because my lips aren't taking orders from my brain. I simply stare. I feel light-headed. I'm not getting enough oxygen.

"Sleep, baby. I'm going to leave now. I'll lock the door behind me. Text me when you wake up in the morning, okay?"

He strokes my cheek until I finally nod. "Yes, Sir." My voice is so soft, I'm not sure he heard it, especially over the ringing in my ears.

One more kiss, and then he leaves. He turns the lights out in my room and in the living room, and then I hear the door close.

He's gone. It feels like a freight train raced through my life and caused a tornado. Pieces of my world are blowing around in the room, spinning like they are caught up in the cyclone. I can't make sense of anything.

I close my eyes and take a deep breath. I'm not sure today was even real. I can't process anything. Brunch... The Olympic Sculpture Park... Shopping... Dinner... Edge... Oh, God. Easton took over. He stripped me naked and made me come. He strapped me to that fancy bench, spanked me, and made me come again so hard I saw stars.

I'm naked in my bed because he's so controlling that even back in my apartment, he was still bossing me around. He's subtle about it, but he does it. He's a Dominant.

He's my Dominant?

That part is baffling. Is he serious? He intends to see me again? I mean, his words insinuated so, but at no point during the day did I allow myself to believe I would see

137

him after today. It's preposterous. I'm not his style. I'm awkward and antisocial. Usually, I can't have much of a conversation with anyone outside of my lab.

When I'm at work, it's easy. Everything I say is for a reason. It's related to my job and the work we're doing. Plus, I think most of the people I work with are just as awkward as me.

Except Trinity. She's normal. If there is such a thing.

When I'm not at work with other equally awkward scientists, I'm a fish out of water. I do what needs to be done outside my apartment—things like grocery shopping or exercising—but I don't look people in the eye. I don't address them. I don't socialize.

Regular humans make me nervous. They have nefarious plans. Most of the people I work with are just like me. They were all probably nerdy and bullied in high school. We don't talk about each other and poke fun. We don't trip each other on the way to the lunch room. We don't intentionally stumble and spill things down someone's shirt.

Trinity has convinced me to go out sometimes to the movies or dinner—and the biggest stretch of all, the kink club. How did I find myself so turned on by that trip to Edge? So much so that I'm the one who returned, and I haven't even told Trinity.

She's going to freak when she finds out what has happened to me. I'm not ready to tell her. I'll keep this to myself for now. I'm not sure I even believe it. I pinch myself, but the movement also reminds me I'm naked. There's no way I would have gotten into bed naked, which means either I was in a trance or Easton really was here in my apartment. He really did strip me down, brush my teeth, boss me around, and tuck me into bed. He really did take my vibrator.

I close my eyes and breathe deeply. I'm exhausted. Too exhausted to continue pondering this massive earthquake that is my life. Tomorrow, I'll be sharper and better able to analyze what has happened.

# CHAPTER 13

FAYE

I jolt awake, gasping as if I haven't taken a breath in a while. For a moment, I stare at the ceiling. I'm definitely in my apartment. Something feels off, though.

I sit upright as I realize the sun is shining. I'm panting as if I've been running, and when the covers drop to my lap, I gasp and look down. Why am I naked?

I jerk my gaze to the clock. Ten? How is that possible? I never sleep this late. My entire routine for the day will be off. Why didn't my alarm go off?

I grab my phone from the nightstand and tap the screen. There's a text.

*Oh. My. God.*

Easton.

> Just making sure you're okay, baby. I hope you're still sleeping. I turned your ringer off so nothing could bother you. Let me know when you wake up.

Easton Riley. He's texting me.

Everything slams into me at once as my memory returns. I was with him all day yesterday. Twelve hours. I went to his club.

*Oh, God...*

Visions swim through my head—too many to follow. I can't focus. I was naked. I wore a skimpy negligée. I jerk my gaze toward my bathroom. If it's real, the bag holding that thin swatch of material is in there.

Easton restrained me to the wall. He made me come. He did it again on the spanking bench. He spanked me. Does my butt hurt?

I throw the covers back, groaning as I stare down at my naked body. How did I let him talk me into sleeping without PJs? The man is a bulldozer. He manages to get his way on everything.

I slide to the floor, and my breath hitches when I glance at my nightstand. The drawer is open slightly, and I yank it all the way open.

Palming my face, I groan. He took my vibrator! The bossy man put it in his pocket and took it!

I slam the drawer shut and stomp toward the bathroom. Before I pee, I turn on the shower. After I pee, I pause at the full-length mirror behind the door and back up to it, looking over my shoulder. At least there's no evidence I was spanked. Maybe at least that part didn't happen. *Yeah, right.*

I brush my teeth next and then climb into the shower before it finishes heating, hoping the cool water will jar me out of my weird state of mind. At least I don't feel drugged like I did last night, but I'm still out of body.

I drop the shampoo bottle when I pick it up, and after

I wash and condition my hair, I can't keep a grip on the bar of soap either. My fingers aren't working. I'm shaking.

When I finally step out of the shower, I'm not fixed. I'm still confused. I'm dripping wet. I usually dry off in the shower. Not on the mat. I'm making a mess of the floor.

I snag my towel and rub my body down, but my hair is soaked. I didn't start with my hair. I'm completely discombobulated.

Somehow, I manage to pat my hair dry and wrap the towel around me before padding back into my room. I need clothes.

I nearly jump out of my skin when a knock at my door is followed immediately by the doorbell. Who would be at my apartment at this hour?

Oh, right. Half the morning is gone. Anyone could be at the door. Except people do not come to my door. The only person who has ever been to my apartment is Trinity, and she would not show up unannounced.

My phone lights up on my nightstand, and I head toward it as it occurs to me who must be at the door.

Sure enough, the incoming text is from Easton.

> Are you awake, Faye? I'm worried. Open the door.

I spin around and hurry toward the door, peeking through the peephole before unlocking it and opening it.

Easton is standing in the frame, taking up more than his share of space. He looks worried, but his shoulders relax as he meets my gaze. "You're okay."

"I'm fine," I lie. "What are you doing here?" I glance down and groan. I'm wrapped in nothing but a towel. My hair isn't even combed, and it's hanging in long, damp ringlets around my shoulders.

"May I come in, Faye?"

I step back.

He enters and shuts the door behind him before cupping my face and leaning down to kiss me. The kiss is deep and consuming. It scatters my already scattered brain. My knees weaken.

Easton catches me with an arm around my waist before I collapse. "You're suffering from sub drop, baby." He bends down, sweeps me off my feet, and carries me cradled into my bedroom.

"What's sub drop?"

"It's what I warned you about. It's why I was worried and came here. I shouldn't have left you alone last night. Did you sleep?"

"Like the dead," I tell him as he stands me on my feet next to my bed.

"Good. You need more rest, though." He yanks my towel away, lifts me by the hips, and manhandles me back into bed. He pulls the covers up my body immediately.

"What are you doing?"

"You need fluid, food, and rest."

"I'm fine." I try to sit up, holding the blanket to my chest.

Mr. Dominant gently pushes me back to the pillows before crowding over me with his hands on either side of my head. "Stay here. I don't know how you even managed to shower. Let me find something for you to eat and drink."

When he rises, I push up again.

He shoots me a glare. "I don't want to spank you again

this morning, but if you continue to test me, I will. It won't end in an orgasm, either."

I gasp.

"Do you want to test me, baby?"

I shake my head.

"Lie down. Don't move."

I lower to my back, panting.

He disappears from my room, leaving me more baffled than I was when I first woke up. He's so bossy.

I squeeze my legs together and slide my hands to my breasts. They feel heavy. My nipples ache as though they've been hard for hours. He pinched them last night. Is that why they're sore?

"What are you doing, Faye?"

A slight scream escapes my lips at the sound of Easton's voice as he re-enters the room. He seems to be fighting a grin as he sets a glass of orange juice and a plate of toast on my nightstand.

I'm frozen, caught with my hands on my boobs. Mortified.

He pulls the covers down to my waist, circles my wrists with his fingers, and pulls my hands from where they're covering my breasts. "I guess I wasn't specific enough last night. When I said no masturbating, I should've included your amazing tits. You may not touch them either. You're so responsive you could probably orgasm from playing with your nipples."

My face heats a thousand degrees, and I squeeze my eyes closed, willing this to not be happening. Every breath makes me aware my chest is bare. He's holding my arms above my head now.

"Look at me, Faye."

I shake my head.

He chuckles. "Baby...look at me."

I take a deep breath and open my eyes because it's impossible to disobey him. My lips are sealed shut.

"I didn't mean to barge in here and dominate the hell out of you. I was worried. You hadn't texted me yet."

I part my lips and lick them. "You *are* dominating the hell out of me," I point out.

"That's because you're irresistible and so fucking submissive." He's still holding me down. I'm still naked. My breasts are rising and falling. I'm aware I have no makeup on, and my hair is a tangled mess. I look dead when I'm not wearing mascara. I'm sure it was all over my face last night when he tucked me in, but I washed it off in the shower.

With a growl, he drops his face down to my neck and nuzzles me until I squirm. He then kisses a path to my lips and kisses me again. I'm not even fully awake, and he's kissing me senseless for a second time.

When he finally releases me—both my lips and my wrists—he pops up to sitting and runs a hand through his hair. After another long look at me, he shoves the covers down to my hips, grabs me around the waist, and pulls me up to sit. He tucks all my pillows behind me to prop me up and reaches for the glass of juice.

I yank the covers up to my neck.

He tugs them back down. "Leave the blankets alone. Drink." He holds out the glass.

I glare at him. Yes, it's hot when he dominates me. Really, really, really hot. I'm sure I have a fever, and my pussy is soaked. But I can't think like this. I need him to back off. "Do I need to use that safeword you made me choose?"

He sucks in a breath, sets the glass on the nightstand, and leans back several inches.

"Get me a shirt, Easton." I point toward the dresser. "Second drawer."

I'm almost surprised when he immediately stands, shuffles toward my dresser, and grabs me a white T-shirt. I'm doubly surprised when he hands it to me when he returns instead of ordering me to lift my arms so he can put it on me himself.

I feel marginally more in control after I lower the shirt over my head, and I try not to worry about the glimpse of my pussy he gets as I slide off the side of the bed before I can pull the long shirt over my butt.

I grab the plate and the glass and walk right past him, heading for the kitchen.

He follows me silently, and when I sit at my usual spot at the table, he sits across from me.

"I don't eat in bed," I tell him as I lift the toast to my lips. I take a bite, staring at him.

He nods, giving me a slight smile. "Of course you don't. I should've thought of that."

"I told you I'm an odd bird, Easton. You're in my apartment. Have you noticed how immaculate I am?"

"Yes." He leans his elbows on the table.

I drink the juice—all of it without stopping, just now realizing how thirsty I am. I'm trying not to freak out over the time and the fact that I missed the breakfast window, and I shouldn't eat at this hour because it will spoil my lunch. I ate at weird times yesterday, too. It's almost like I'm a normal woman.

Ha.

Reality seeps in as I finish my toast. I'm not going to be able to skip having tea, so I shove my chair back and pad over to the counter to turn on the kettle. While it heats, I grab a mug and a teabag. I spin around. "I don't have coffee. Would you like some tea?"

"No, baby. I'm fine."

I draw in a breath. He keeps using that endearment with me as if it were possible I could ever be his baby. It's not. I can't be what he needs. I had fun yesterday, but I'm not girlfriend material. He spoke of me coming to the club often and sleeping in his bed. I can't do those things. My routine is a hot mess after just one day. I'm shaking as I think about everything I didn't do yesterday and what I haven't done today.

I face away from him, grab the counter, and close my eyes. Deep breaths. I have a therapist because I'm self-aware, and I need her to help talk me off these kinds of ledges, but I've never stood on a ledge this high. She won't even believe this. Even if I only tell her one-tenth of what happened this weekend, she will think I've been taken over by an alien. I'm not sure that isn't what has happened.

My own personal crazy is about to surface, and I'm not going to hold it back because Easton needs to understand what I'm like.

The kettle boils. I pour the water into my mug and set it back down. When I return to the table, Easton has not moved. He's watching me closely.

I'm in control here. He has pulled back. Thank God.

I sit and take several sips of the tea, grateful that my brain starts to kick in. Finally, I set the mug down and look at him. "I have obsessive tendencies, Easton."

"I know, Faye. You told me."

"You have no idea how out of my element I am right now. I keep a strict schedule. I haven't followed it for twenty-four hours. I'm self-aware enough to know that nothing on my schedule needed to be done. It won't matter that I skipped cleaning my toilet yesterday or didn't do a load of whites. It won't be the end of the world that my bed isn't made even though I left the room or that I ate toast at ten thirty in the morning. I won't die from not reading from nine to ten or jogging from eight to eight forty-five. I know that, but you need to understand those are the kinds of things I normally do on a schedule, and I'm confused and shaken from not doing them."

He doesn't interrupt me, and when I'm done, he nods. "I hear you, Faye."

I find myself giggling out of nowhere. "You've had counseling, too." No one listens to another person so intently and then validates their feelings like that without extensive counseling of their own.

He shrugs. "How do you think I managed to convert myself from that geeky, scrawny kid in high school to a man people pay attention to? Yes, I had a lot of counseling. I'm not ignorant about what makes people tick."

"So, you can understand me when I say there is no way this thing between us..." I wave a hand back and forth, "...can possibly become a habit."

He shakes his head. "I disagree with you there. It's too late. This *thing* is already a habit."

I draw in a sharp breath. "We've known each other for like...one day."

"I only needed one hour. By the time we finished brunch, I knew I wanted you."

I should be grateful he's honest. But I'm freaking out. I sip some more tea, but it doesn't help me calm down. I set the mug down before I drop it. I'm sitting in my kitchen in nothing but a T-shirt with my bare butt on the chair. I'm not sure I've ever been out of my room without being dressed.

"We're so different," I point out.

"But we want the same thing, and we're madly attracted to each other." He leans back, looking confident. He even crosses his arms. "We'll work out the details, Faye, but don't turn away from this."

"How can you feel so confident?"

"I'm thirty-five years old. I've dated a lot of women. I've dominated dozens. I've had several semi-long-term girlfriends. I've never felt like this."

My breath hitches. I cross my arms and fiddle with the neck of my T-shirt.

He leans forward again, sets his elbows on the table, and holds my gaze in that intense way he does. "Drake nearly bit my head off last night for leaving you, especially when I told him how amazing our day was."

I wince.

"Baby, I didn't tell him what we did in my private apartment. Just the big picture. But he didn't need me to tell him how I dominated you. I've never texted him and told him I wouldn't be able to open the club with him. I've never flaked and locked my door and not come out for three hours. I've never taken my finger off the business and left everything to work itself out without even texting or checking my phone. He knew it was important. And it was. Last night was the most powerful night of my life. Tell me it wasn't the same for you."

I swallow hard. It was, but if I admit that...

He ignores my silence. "It's okay if you need time. I'll give you time and space. I understand your foundation is rocked. I know this is huge for you and you're not used to sharing your space or time with another human. I won't pretend it's not more earth-shattering for you because you haven't ever been in *any* relationship, let alone a D/s arrangement. I'll back off and let you collect your thoughts, but don't shut me out."

I bite my lip. I don't know how to respond.

"We have a powerful connection. You know it as well as I do. You will never be happy without kink in your life now that you've tasted it. You need a strong Dominant to help you get the release you crave. I want to be that man. It means making changes to your life. I get that. It might mean we have to work harder than other people to blend our lives. But please open your heart to the possibility."

My lip hurts from biting it.

He draws in another breath. "Will you be okay if I leave you alone, baby? Are you feeling too out-of-sorts still? The sub drop was intense."

I shake my head. "I'm fine now. I just needed a shower and some tea."

He folds his hands under his chin and stares at the table for long seconds. "I'll go so you can get back into your routine. May I please text you?"

I nod. "Yes."

"I might text you often."

I smile. "That's okay. I won't answer when I'm working, though."

"I understand. I will worry about you, so please give me a few words every now and then so I don't panic."

He sounds so vulnerable that it's oddly endearing. He means every word. He really wants to have a relationship with me. I'm stunned to say the least.

When he stands, I do, too. He heads for the door, sets his hand on the knob, and turns toward me. "Think about it, Faye. Please. Think about giving me a chance. Come to the club anytime you want. It's open Wednesday through Saturday."

I nod. I know this.

"Call me if you want to talk. Or text."

"Okay," I whisper.

He opens the door and steps into the hallway. He hesitates a moment, meeting my gaze, but then turns and heads toward the stairs.

I stand in the doorway, watching him until the door to the stairwell shuts. It sounds loud and makes me flinch. I feel heavy as I step back inside and shut the door. For a long time, I stand leaning against it, rubbing my neck with one hand, too shocked to do anything else.

My Sunday routine is shot to hell. When I finally move, I head straight back to my room. I'm chilled, and I head for my closet, shove my clothes to one side, and reach for the navy jacket that hangs in the back. When I put it on, I instantly feel more settled.

It's silly. I've had this jacket since high school. I pull it out in times like this when I'm out of sorts and need comforting. That's what the jacket did for me the day I acquired it, and it still works today.

Wrapped up in the worn, old garment, I climb under the covers as if I were sick. I need more rest. I need to escape.

When I close my eyes, I drift back to that day. I remember it like it was yesterday. It was one of the most humiliating days in my life. I can still hear the laughter coming from all around me as I stood in the middle of the cafeteria with tomato sauce dripping down the front of my blouse.

I couldn't breathe. I was frozen in my spot, unable to

turn and run from the room. My ears were ringing. I wondered how I was going to survive the day.

I pull the front of the jacket up to my nose and inhale. It no longer has a scent, and I no longer remember what it smelled like. I only know that it saved me from further embarrassment. It's a symbol of kindness. A reminder that someone cared about me. I pull this jacket out and wear it every time I need to remember that some humans are good.

It takes me a minute to get comfortable, and then I stare at the ceiling, trying to process everything. It's too much. I'm overwhelmed. I'm glad Easton is gone so I can think. I can't think when he's in my space. I can only obey. But I also hate that he's gone. I like having him near me, touching me, dominating me, taking care of me.

How could I possibly make the kinds of changes he's suggesting? I don't see how I could. I'm too set in my ways to add a man to my life. I like my space. My apartment is exactly how I want it. I get nervous when my routine is broken.

I close my eyes and take deep breaths, curling into myself until I finally fall back to sleep.

# CHAPTER 14

EASTON

"You still haven't spoken to her?" Drake asks.

I drop onto my chair in our shared office as though I weigh two thousand pounds. I feel like it. I'm dragging. During my workout this morning, I felt like I hadn't been to the gym in ten years. "Texts."

"Just texts."

"Yes." I text her twice a day—once in the morning and once at night. I won't let myself text her more often. I don't want her to feel like I'm hovering even though I'm definitely hovering. *Hovering on the edge of panic.*

"Does she return these texts?"

"Yes. Sort of." I run my hand through my hair.

"So, brief answers. One or two words."

"Yep." I pull on my hair now. I might resort to pulling it out.

"And you haven't seen her since Sunday morning?"

I groan. "Yes, Drake. Stop badgering me. I know I'm pitiful."

"Oh, you're way more than pitiful. I'm struggling not to laugh. You told me there was no way you were ready to enter into a new relationship so soon after Bethany. You said you didn't think you would ever be willing to put your heart out there like that again. Faye must be a goddess between the sheets." He shakes his head and turns around.

I wince behind his back. I have no idea what Faye might be like between the sheets, but I won't tell him that. It's not his business. Faye would be pissed if I talked about our sex life with someone else. She would be doubly pissed if I told my brother she was a virgin.

It would shock Drake and make his head explode if he knew I was harboring this kind of lust for a woman I have not even fucked. Though I would never fuck Faye. She deserves to be pampered. The only term for the sex we will have is making love.

Every day has been a roller coaster of emotions. I wake up frustrated and bitchy. I stomp around my home, growling as though my dog died. I don't have a dog. Eileen, my housekeeper, has stopped talking to me. She's been with me for five years. She's the best housekeeper on Earth, but I've caused her to steer clear of me. She finds some other room to work in as soon as I get close.

I've apologized to her and assured her my frustration has nothing to do with her. She purses her lips and nods. I'm confident she thinks my behavior has something to do with a woman, but I refuse to discuss it with her.

"Take the night off," Drake says, not looking back at me.

"I can't do that. It's Friday. The place will be packed. Besides, what would I do? Go home and pace?"

He spins around. "Don't be a dipshit. Go buy the woman some flowers and knock on her door. Make her talk to you. What's the worst that can happen?"

I groan. "She could tell me to go take a fucking hike and never speak to me again." At least now she hasn't cut me off from texting.

"That would be better than what you're going through. At least you'd know. I think you need to get in her face and make her look at you. You're giving her too much space."

Maybe he's right.

"I hate to make it sound like you're unimportant because that's not true, but this place can survive a Friday night without you. I promise. I'll be here. No one has called in sick. It will be fine. We've talked about cutting back on our involvement for months. We both know Edge can run itself. The only reason we still keep our thumbs on every aspect of the business is because we're controlling."

I chuckle. "And we like to play."

"That, too." He points at the door. "Go."

"Okay." I push up from my seat and scoot out the door before he can change his mind, or someone calls with a problem. We aren't even open yet, so it's unlikely there's a problem in the building.

Thirty minutes later, I'm standing at Faye's door with a bouquet of roses in one hand and my heart in the other. This woman has the power to crush me.

I knock and wait. Maybe she's not home. After all, it's Friday night. Duh. She might be out with friends, or what if she decided to go to Edge? Wouldn't it be comical if I were standing here while she was at Edge?

I'm almost surprised when the door opens.

I know several things instantly. One, she's mine. My God, this woman is mine. Any doubt I might have had flees the universe the moment I set eyes on her.

Two, she's so damn gorgeous. It's not that I've forgotten. It's that I'm reminded. She's wearing black leggings and an oversized university sweatshirt. Her hair is in a messy bun on top of her head. She's holding a paperback with one finger marking her page. Her feet are bare. She has on no makeup. She's never been lovelier.

Three, she's not displeased to see me. She's not exasperated. She doesn't sigh or roll her eyes. In fact, she's almost smiling. Thank God. "Hey," she says.

"Hey." I hold out the roses. "I brought you roses."

"I see that. Thank you." She takes a step back, holding the door wider.

I step inside at the silent invitation. "I promised I would give you space, but I couldn't stand not seeing you another minute."

She turns and heads toward the kitchen area, pulls a large glass down from a cabinet, and fills it with water.

I'm baffled until she takes the roses from me and puts them in the water. Duh. Right.

"They're very pretty," she says before she leans closer to smell them. "Mmm. No one has ever brought me roses before."

My chest tightens. "I wasn't sure if you even liked roses or any flowers. Some people don't like the scent."

She smiles. "I love them."

Then I'll buy her roses every week.

I nod toward the book she set on the counter. "I'm interrupting."

She chuckles. "Yes, my scheduled reading hour."

I rub my hands on my thighs. If I waited for a time when I wouldn't interrupt something she scheduled, I think I'd be waiting a lifetime because I'm pretty sure she has every hour of her life planned, including precise moments when she eats, sleeps, and pees.

She turns toward the couch and sits in the corner, pulling her legs up under her. "Do you want to sit?"

I want to do a lot more than sit, but I nod and join her, not sitting too closely but close enough I can touch her if I want. I turn my body sideways so I'm facing her. "I've missed you," I admit.

She turns more fully toward me, pulls her knees up to her chest, and wraps her arms around them. She takes my breath away. "You might find this hard to believe, but I've missed you, too."

*Thank you, God.*

"It's been weird."

"What's been weird?" I ask.

"We only spent one day together. Not even the night, but most of a twenty-four hour period. And yet, I feel different."

"How?"

"I feel...lonely. My apartment is quiet. My books are boring. My bed is half empty. My workouts are pitiful. I feel like I knew you for a really long time, and then you went away and left a hole."

Blessed angels.

I want to touch her, but I don't. I need to tread carefully. "Maybe you need better reading material," I joke.

She giggles.

"And some music. If you had music playing, your apartment would feel more lively. You could listen to it while you work out, too," I propose. "And they sell these body-length pillows you can curl up with in bed. Though I'm not sure why your bed is lonely since I never slept in it." I smile.

She giggles again.

We stare at each other for a long time, both of us grinning like loons.

Finally, she says, "I'm scared."

"I get that. I'm pretty fucking scared, myself," I admit.

"You? I can't believe you're ever scared."

I shake my head. "Baby, I've been scared since I first set eyes on you."

"Of what?"

"Of falling too hard. Of getting hurt. Of hurting you unintentionally. Of doing something that would scare you away. Of not seeing your face every day of my life. The list is long."

She bites her lip. I love it when she bites that lip. I want to bite it, too.

"Tell me why *you're* scared," I encourage.

She draws in a slow breath. "I'm scared of losing myself, of not being capable of sharing my life, of doing something stupid that makes you turn away from me, of making a fool of myself, of getting hurt when this ends, and probably ten other things."

"What if it didn't end?"

She shrugs. "Everything ends."

"Not everything."

"Relationships do. I don't think I know one person who has stayed with their partner forever. I observe the relationship ritual at work over and over again. At first, it's all sunshine and roses. Someone comes in on a Monday morning, mooning over whoever they went out with over the weekend. They have stars in their eyes for days, and then the stars dull, and eventually, they realize the person they've been infatuated with is not quite right for them. Maybe they were even married. Sometimes for years. It always ends."

"Not every relationship ends, Faye. Some stay together. My parents love each other, and they're still together."

Her eyebrows rise. "Really? Where do they live?"

"They live in France." I chuckle. "When my dad retired, they moved to the coast of France. Apparently, it had been a dream of theirs. We still see them once a year, but they're living the dream."

"You're also living the dream," she points out. "Not many thirty-five-year-old men have developed and sold as many apps as you and your brother have."

I shrug. "The dream isn't very fun if you don't have someone to share it with." I tentatively hold out a hand. "Share it with me, Faye. Take a chance."

She releases her legs with one hand and sets her palm in mine. "The thought makes me panic. I don't trust easily."

I arch an eyebrow. "And how do you feel when you consider telling me to take a hike and not seeing me again?"

She swallows. "Worse."

"Then do you really have a choice?"

She smiles. "Not really."

"Would you have eventually called or come to the club if I hadn't shown up tonight?"

"Yeah...I was pretty impressed that you lasted this long."

I narrow my gaze at her. "Were you testing me?" I rub her knuckles.

"No." She shakes her head. "It's just that you consume me. I knew as soon as I broke down, I would get sucked into your world and never come back up for air. I needed some time to evaluate my life and talk to my therapist."

"Oh. You told her about me?"

"Yes."

"How much did you tell her?"

"Surprisingly, most of it. She knew a lot about the kink world, so she didn't flinch as I reiterated my day with you."

"And what did she think you should do?"

"For a long time, she simply nodded and let me talk. And then she was really quiet for a while. Nervous. She kept tapping her pen on her paper. I was about to freak out when she finally told me she knew you."

My eyes widen. "She knows me?"

"Yeah, she didn't tell me how, but considering how much she seemed to know about the kink community, I assume she's a member of Edge. She felt awkward because it affected her ability to be impartial, but she told me you were one of the best men she knew and that I couldn't go wrong if I gave you a chance."

I'm stunned. Who is this woman? It's possible she's a member of Edge, and that she knows me, but I have no idea who she is. "What's her name, Faye?"

"Olivia Black."

I chuckle and then start laughing.

"What's so funny?"

"She's my counselor, too. I haven't seen her for a while, but if I ever needed someone again, she would be my go-to. What a small world."

"Wow. Crazy. I guess she couldn't tell me that. Client privacy and all. So, she's not a member of Edge?"

"No. That would probably be awkward for her since I'm one of the owners. If she belongs to a kink club, it's another one. There are several others in the area. Drake and I are both members of two other clubs—Surrender and The Playground. We never go to them anymore since we have our own, but the point is they exist." I scoot closer and lift her hand to my cheek.

She stares at me, smiling. "Well, since she did endorse you..."

"What if she hadn't?"

"I would've eventually sought you out because you stole my vibrator, and I want it back."

I laugh. "I'm not giving it back."

"Why not? You can't seriously think you can control my orgasms." She says this as though she's incensed.

I rub her knuckles against my cheek. "I *can* control your orgasms. All of them. Did you masturbate this week?" I know she didn't. She can't break rules. It's not in her nature.

She sighs. "No, but I wanted to."

"What did you wear to bed?"

"My pajamas," she retorts as if I'm batshit for suggesting otherwise.

"What a shame." I grin at her. This is going better than I expected. I'm starting to think I might have a chance with this amazing woman.

"So now what?" she asks.

"What was on your Friday night agenda?"

BECCA JAMESON

She looks away and then back at me. "I was going to stare at that book for a while, pretending to read it so I could account for the number of pages, when really what I was doing was thinking of the pros and cons of seeing you again. I thought about texting or calling. I thought about showing up at the club."

"Will you spend the evening with me?"

She licks her lips. "Here?"

"Anywhere. Here. My place. The club. A combination of those."

She chews on her lip this time, thinking. "Will you take me to the second floor?" she asks softly.

"Absolutely. Will you submit to me?"

She nods.

"Will you come home with me after?"

"To your place?"

"Yes."

"Do you have one of those full-body pillows I can try out?"

I slowly smile at her joke. She has a dry humor that sneaks out now and then. "No. I have something better."

"Can I have my vibrator back?"

"No, but you can use it if you let me watch."

Her cheeks pinken. I love it when she gets all shy with me. It's adorable. "I'm not sure I could do that."

"You could if I instructed you to." I lift a brow. "Submission is in your blood."

"Yeah, you're probably right." She sighs. "The only thing I have to wear to the club is the same negligée I wore last week. I washed it, though."

"That's perfect. No one even saw it."

Her face turns a darker pink before she says, "I don't have a thong. Someone cut it off my body."

I chuckle. "Then I guess you'll have to go naked underneath."

Her breath hitches. "Scandalous."

I kiss her fingers. "Go change, baby."

She hesitates. "Here? Shouldn't I change at the club?"

"Nope. You can do it here. You can put those leggings on underneath and a coat. When we get there, you'll remove everything but the negligée." I scoot forward and help her stand. "Pack several things in an overnight bag, too. You're not coming back here tonight."

She shuffles toward her bedroom.

"Faye?"

"Yes, Sir?"

*Oh yes. Damn.* "Don't wear panties."

# CHAPTER 15

FAYE

I'm not as nervous as I enter the club this time. Or maybe I'm just as nervous, but it's for a different reason. I don't have the first-time jitters I had for the intro class. I also don't have the panicked feeling I had last Saturday when I came here, uncertain what Easton might ask of me.

This time, I have a pretty good idea of what he will expect me to do. The question is, will I like it?

He guides me to the third floor and into his private lair. I like thinking of it as a lair. "Take everything off except the sexy black silk, Faye," he commands. "Put your clothes on the bed."

I head toward the bathroom.

He stops me. "No, baby. Do it in front of me. You're not ever changing in another room again. From now on, I will watch you dress and undress. Sometimes, I will do it myself."

I nod and head for the bed. I shouldn't be surprised. I

shouldn't really care, either. He's seen all of me. What does it matter now?

On the other hand, I haven't even seen his chest. We are very unbalanced in this area. "When will I see you naked?" I ask as I put my coat on the bed.

"When I decide you're ready."

"Are you going to sleep with me tonight?" I ask.

"I'm going to sleep in the same bed with you, yes. I won't be naked until I think you're ready."

"Don't you think a thirty-one-year-old woman is about a decade past ready?"

He chuckles. "Nope. My cock stays in my pants until I decide to take it out. Don't ask again."

I kick off my shoes and then stare directly at him as I reach under the hem of the silk to push my leggings down my thighs. I'm deliberately teasing him, which is way out of my wheelhouse but seems to come naturally when I'm with him.

When I finish, I look at him. He nods. "Come." He heads for the attached bathroom.

I follow him.

He carefully takes my hair down from the messy bun, grabs a brush, and gently works out the tangles until it lays in long curls down my back. He sets the brush down and kisses my neck. "Sometimes, I will want it up when we play, so I don't accidentally pull it and hurt you, but tonight, I'm not going to do anything that would possibly cause your hair to get trapped."

What *is* he going to do tonight? I'm at a loss but curious.

He takes my hand and guides me from the room.

"Do I need shoes?"

"No, baby. I like you barefoot. We keep the floors very

clean on the second and third floors. Lots of submissives are barefoot."

With our fingers threaded together, he guides me into his office.

Drake is there, and he spins around. His face lights up when he sees us. "Faye. So good to see you."

"Hi," I whisper. I'm embarrassed to be standing in front of Easton's twin, wearing this scandalously skimpy negligée, but I'm certain far more people are about to see it both on and off me in the next hour, so I need to rein in my angst.

Easton steps behind me and sets his hands on my shoulders. He slides his palms down my arms, clasps my hands, and pulls them around to my back. His lips come to my ear. "Clasp one wrist with the other hand, baby."

I shiver as I do as he says. The position thrusts my breasts forward.

"Good girl. Part your legs a few inches and wait for me while I check on a few things."

I obey his command, feeling extremely exposed already. The only person seeing me is Drake, and he's not really seeing anything. Except for my nipples. There's no way to avoid the hard points pressing against the silk.

Easton sits at his computer, gives the mouse a shake, and proceeds to intently look at something. I suspect his only intention is to see how I will react.

Drake smiles. "I hear you're going to do a scene on the second floor."

I'm unsure how I'm expected to address Drake, but I say, "Yes, Sir."

His smile broadens. "You don't have to call me Sir, Faye, unless it makes you more comfortable. Sometimes, submissives speak reverently to everyone around when

BECCA JAMESON

they're in that headspace. Unless Easton prefers you call me Sir, you may call me Drake."

I nod. "Okay."

"There." Easton spins around. "I just popped an email to Barbara from Kink Outfitters. She's going to send some more apparel for you to my house." He grins evilly.

I bite my lip. "Sounds dangerous."

He pushes up from his seat and glances at Drake. "We're going downstairs. Don't need me."

Drake chuckles. "No problem. Enjoy."

When we step into the hallway, Easton rounds in front of me, cups my face, and kisses me. It's sensual and rocks my world, but he doesn't take it too deep. He keeps it light. "You okay?"

"Yes, Sir."

"Safeword?"

"Liver, Sir."

"Remember, the universal safeword is always *red*. Any club monitor will intervene if they hear *red*. Use the word *yellow* if you need me to slow down, pause, check in with you, or if you just need to catch your breath."

"Yes, Sir."

"Good girl. Ready?"

I'm not sure I could ever be ready for whatever we're about to do, but the new Faye, who has apparently taken over my body, wants to experience anything Easton throws at me. "Yes, Sir."

He clasps my hand and leads me down to the second floor. As we pass Marny, she waves at us. "Have fun."

The club is in full swing when we step inside. Most of the apparatuses are being used. I'm confused when Easton guides me to the center of the room. The only thing I see is a black mat, like the kind a gymnast would use. It's soft under my feet, but what are we going to do here?

Several people turn around and watch as Easton slowly circles me. He speaks in his seductive, commanding voice. "Hands clasped behind your back, Faye. Spread your feet wider."

I easily comply since this is the position he just had me in upstairs. I'm sure he was preparing me for this moment.

More people gather in a circle around me. It's unnerving. I don't know why they would want to watch me standing here in this submissive position. It's not interesting.

Easton steps closer, leans into my ear, and whispers, "Feel their gazes on you. You're so sexy."

I tremble.

He pulls something out of his pocket. Some kind of remote. When he pushes a button, I hear the sound of some sort of machinery moving. It's coming from above, and I tip my head back to see an apparatus descending from the high ceiling.

My heart rate picks up as it gets closer, and he stops it a foot above my head.

"Lift your arms, baby," he whispers in my ear.

I suck in a breath and do as I'm told, knowing he's going to attach me to this apparatus over my head and make me feel instantly more vulnerable. I'm bare beneath this tiny silky negligée. I'm also already wet. It will rise. People will see my naked pussy in a few seconds.

Easton slides his hand from my armpit to my wrist and encircles it with a soft cuff. He then pulls my arm slightly higher and attaches me to an eye hook at the end of a bar. When he comes around to do the same on my other side, I start panting.

I can feel the swish of silk around my bottom and hips. The negligée didn't do much to hide my assets, but it's doing less now. For the first time in my life, I'm extremely exposed. Dozens of people have gathered.

Easton's lips come to my ear as he cups my neck. "They can only see a hint of your pretty pussy so far, baby. It's a tease. They'd have to bend down to really get a look at your pussy or the slightest swell of your perfect bottom. I'm going to put a bar between your feet now. Stay still for me."

I'm conscious of every noise coming from my mouth. The room is hushed because it's impolite to speak above a whisper while scenes are going on.

I tip my head back and look up at my wrists while Easton attaches my ankles to the spreader bar. It's not super wide. Just wide enough to keep me from squeezing my thighs together. Just wide enough to make me feel exposed.

When he's done, he slides his hands up my legs, flicking the hem of my negligée up when he reaches my hips. It's just a flash for the crowd, but it makes my breath hitch and my body tense.

He circles behind me and sets his palms on my waist on top of the silk next. His lips come to my ear. "You're so fucking sexy. Everyone is squirming. Look at them."

I whimper. I don't want to look at the people watching me. I shake my head defiantly.

He shifts his hands to my breasts and pinches both my nipples hard enough to bring me to my toes. "Look at their faces, Faye. I want you to see the lust in their gazes so you'll know how fucking hot you are."

"Please..." I try to squirm free of the firm grip he has on my nipples. It's painful.

"I'll release them after you do as you were told, baby." His breath against my neck drives me mad with need.

I lower my gaze and force myself to scan the faces in front of me. Dozens. They are all silent and still... intrigued, horny. He's right.

"Good girl." He releases my aching buds and circles them with his pointers, making me squirm. "In a moment, I'm going to pull these cups down so everyone can see your gorgeous tits. You want them to see how pretty they are, don't you?"

"Yes, Sir," I breathe.

"No one will ever be permitted to touch them but me. I want them to be jealous of what's mine." His voice is deep and soft. It's only for my ears. Every syllable is uttered against my neck, tickling me, making me want more.

He keeps circling my nipples. They're harder than ever and ache deliciously.

Finally, he trails his fingers along the edge of the V between my breasts instead, teasing my skin until I'm covered with goosebumps. He reaches under the lace and flicks my nipples. "Look at your audience, baby. Watch their expressions as I expose your breasts."

I'm panting as I obey him, letting my gaze fall on one woman in particular who's standing in my line of sight. She has her arms crossed, and she's stroking her neck with her fingers. I'm making her horny.

The lace drags over my swollen buds as Easton pulls the cups down. I arch and writhe as he exposes me to everyone in the room. It's so heady. My adrenaline is pumping. I can't believe I'm doing this. Letting a Dom bare my breasts while I'm restrained and helpless.

My full breasts are pushed up by the silky cups now resting under them. Easton lightly touches them, tormenting my nipples, tapping them, circling them, flicking them.

I moan.

"That's a good girl. Show them how good it feels to be touched by me. How good it feels to have all these people looking at your amazing tits."

I arch my chest forward, unable to control my body's reactions.

"Is your pussy dripping, baby?"

"Yes, Sir," I whisper. It's running down my inner thighs. I'm sure some people can see it.

"Do you want me to touch your folds?"

I ponder his question. Is there a right or wrong answer? Does it matter? I'm desperate. "Please, Sir." I don't care that so many people are watching. I want him to stroke my clit. I need to come so badly.

Leaving the cups obscenely tucked under my boobs, he flattens one palm on my tummy and lowers the other to the hem of my negligée. His fingers dance against my inner thigh for a moment before he drags them quickly through my folds and across my clit.

I cry out, the sound shocking me.

"So gorgeous, Faye. You're driving the room mad with lust."

He removes his fingers so fast, leaving me desperate and panting. "Please..."

"Not here, baby. You will not come while everyone watches. Let them look. Let them feel jealous. Save your orgasm for me."

"Yes, Sir." I whimper because I need to come so badly I don't care who watches. But I do care about obeying Easton. He doesn't want to share my orgasms, and that makes me feel special.

He circles to my front, his hands never leaving my body. Now, they're sitting on my hips again, but he's pulling me against his chest. He holds my gaze and says nothing as he uses his fingers to gather up the few inches of silk at my bottom and lifts it slowly until my ass is exposed to the entire room.

I'm confused when he starts slowly turning us in a circle, and I tip my head back to see that the device I'm attached to spins. He's letting everyone in the room see my ass.

It's hard to shuffle my feet with the bar attached to my ankles, but I manage, keeping my balance because his hands are holding me.

After he makes a full circle, he stops and pulls the material up higher. "Eyes on mine, baby."

I hold his gaze, my mouth hanging open. My breaths are shallow, and I give a little gasp when I realize he has exposed my pussy entirely. I'm standing so close to him that most people can't fully see the front, but with my legs parted, they can see a lot from the back.

"Let them look at what's mine," he whispers. "They're so jealous."

I purse my lips. I'm so exposed. I hear whispers around the room. They're talking about me. What are they saying?

For a moment I panic. I'm dragged back to high school. I squeeze my eyes shut, remembering everyone taunting me in the cafeteria that day. It's hard to shake the feeling, but I force myself to return to the present.

These people are not being unkind. They are jealous. I'm no longer a skinny, gangly teenager with a flat chest, stringy red hair, and no sense of style. I'm a grown adult. I'm sexy. I have nice breasts. My hair is styled well. Yes, people are whispering, but they are jealous.

As if he reads my mind, Easton says, "They think you're so sexy. They're wishing they had the nerve to expose themselves like this. The women are hot and bothered, as if they're experiencing this exposure instead of you. Remember how you felt that first night watching Doms unveil their subs for everyone to see?"

I nod.

He smiles. "When we're done, you're coming home with me. No one will watch as I spread you out on my bed, open your legs, and eat your pussy until you scream. No one will hear you but me."

Easton releases the silk, letting it fall around me. He steps back and returns to stand behind me again. Cupping my breasts, he whispers in my ear. "Are you turned on?"

"Yes, Sir."

"Can you take more?"

I tremble. "Yes, Sir."

"Do you want everyone to see how wet you are, how needy and salacious?"

I shudder. "Yes, Sir." There's something incredibly powerful in knowing that I've mesmerized dozens of people with my wanton body. It makes me feel sexy, and I've never felt sexy until I came to Edge. It never occurred to me that I could be sexy. It's powerful.

He pulls something out of his pocket, and I flinch when something cold touches my shoulder. I glance just in time to watch him snip the spaghetti strap holding up the negligée. A second later, he cuts the other side.

The entire negligée falls to the floor, leaving me totally naked.

I tip my head back and moan. I can't look at anyone. I prefer to visualize their stunned expressions in my head. Am I really as sexy as Easton insists I am? It was one thing to have them catch a glimpse of my pussy and a flash of ass. They saw my breasts pushed up with the cups of my negligée. However, now, I'm naked. The entire package. So very exposed.

Easton separates my hair at my back and drapes it over my shoulders so that it falls in waves across my chest, shrouding my breasts in a strawberry-blond curtain.

He stops touching me and steps back to slowly circle me. "Arch your chest, baby. Let your nipples peek out."

His words make me arch. I don't even need the command. The tone alone is enough. The feel of my hair sliding along the sides of my naked breasts is sensual. My nipples stiffen harder as though he's touching them.

When he's at my back, he steps away for a moment and returns with something in his hand. He comes to my front and shows it to me.

My breath hitches. It's a crop. I panic a bit because I'm unprepared for the addition of impact play.

"I'm not going to strike you, Faye. You have my word. I'm going to tease your skin with the leather flap." He brings it to my stomach and drags the folded flap of leather across my waist.

I whimper.

Easton trails it up and lets the tip flick over my nipple next.

I rise onto my toes. I'm stunned by how many things

he can do to me to make me horny. He's not even touching me directly. He's using a small piece of leather, and my arousal is growing.

He steps close to whisper in my ear, "Say yellow if you get too close to orgasm. You're not allowed to come."

"Yes, Sir."

Easton uses the other end of the crop to part my hair away from my breasts before flipping it around again and stroking the undersides of my breasts.

The globes are high and full with my arms over my head. I suppose they're nice to look at, but they're slightly large for my small waist and frame.

Easton rounds to my back again, dragging the leather flap along my skin and then down my spine until he trails it between my ass cheeks.

I clench my cheeks together and arch forward to avoid the embarrassing touch so close to my rectum.

He stays behind me, drawing circles on my bottom and down to my thighs. When he trails the crop up between my legs, I moan involuntarily. I'm torn. I want him to touch my pussy, while at the same time, I'm afraid I will break his rule and orgasm. Not to mention how embarrassing it would be to orgasm in front of all the people from the simple touch of a crop.

He comes close but doesn't touch my folds before leaning in from behind to whisper, "Scale of one to ten— how close are you to orgasm?"

"Seven, Sir."

"Good girl." He rounds to my front and torments the tops of my thighs. Holding my gaze, he teases precariously close to my pussy.

"Yellow," I cry out, the word echoing in the room. I'm throbbing with need.

He lowers the crop. "Good girl." He threads a hand in my hair, holds my head, and leans his forehead against mine. "Such a good girl."

I feel like his good girl. I feel needy and sexy. I want to come.

"Have you had enough, Faye?"

I nod. I think I have. I'm losing the ability to hold myself up. My palms are wrapped around the leather above them, holding on, but I'm growing weak.

"Good girl. I'm so proud of you." He drops the crop, then reaches up and releases my wrists. In seconds, he has my ankles unfastened, too. He wraps a soft blanket around my body, picks me up, snuggles me securely against him, and walks away from the scene.

I burrow my face in his neck, half aware that he carries me out of the room and up the stairs to the third floor. I'm relieved and exhausted—and still so horny that my pussy is pulsing between my thighs.

# CHAPTER 16

## EASTON

When I pull into the garage behind my home, Faye is sound asleep. She fell asleep the moment I buckled her in. The scene we did was extremely intense. I had intended to give her an orgasm afterward in the privacy of my third-floor apartment, but she was exhausted and unable to focus. An orgasm wouldn't have been consensual.

I lift her into my arms and carry her limp body into my house. I will have to give her a tour tomorrow. She's dead weight tonight.

Luckily, Drake took one look at Faye and told me to take her home. Bless him. One of these days, he'll meet his dream woman, and I will return the favor.

I also texted Eileen earlier and told her to take tomorrow off. Eileen is a gem, the best housekeeper on earth. She works full-time, making sure everything is taken care of in my home. I'm spoiled. The best part is that she's an amazing cook. She makes all my meals. She even makes everything I will need to eat on weekends and puts it in containers in my fridge.

On Saturdays, she usually comes in for just a few hours to make sure I'm fed. It's not necessary, but again, she's a gem.

Faye would probably freak if another person is in the house when she wakes up tomorrow. This is for the best.

I carry her upstairs and consider giving her a bath, but she's too tired, and no one but me touched her. Before we left the club, I set her on the counter in the bathroom of my apartment to wash her feet.

Faye was so out of it that she didn't complain as I dressed her in a T-shirt, leggings, socks, and shoes. I helped her into her coat and carried her down to my car.

Now that I've reached my bedroom, I drop her overnight bag on the floor, pull her coat off, tug the covers back, and lower her onto the mattress.

She whimpers adorably. This woman cannot possibly scene more than once a week. It wipes her out. And there is no way I would take her to the club on a weeknight. She'd never make it to work the next day.

She fusses a bit without opening her eyes as I undress her, but I want her naked in my bed. Hell, I want her naked in my bed for the rest of my damn life.

It's scary how strongly I feel about Faye. No wonder no previous relationship of mine worked out. I've never felt this way about a woman. I can't believe that just a few weeks ago, I was actually depressed over my breakup with Bethany. I realize now I was mostly just frustrated that I'd so poorly misjudged Bethany. We weren't a good fit, which I knew for a while. I wasn't exactly surprised when we called it quits. It was mutual. We couldn't see eye-to-eye.

What would have happened if I'd still been in a relationship with another woman when Faye walked through the door of Edge? I shudder.

I quickly slide Faye's naked body to the middle of the bed and pull the covers over her. She stops whimpering and snuggles into a ball on her side, breathing easier once she's cozy.

I don't want to leave her for long because she might wake up confused, so I hurry to brush my teeth and grab a tall glass of water. I made her drink a bottle before we left Edge, but she will wake up hungover again.

After turning out the lights and stripping down to my boxer briefs, I climb into bed and gently manhandle Faye until she's where I want her—spooned against my chest.

I inhale her scent, the vanilla shampoo she uses, her soap, and the rest is Faye. I'll never get enough of her, which scares me to death.

It's going to take some convincing to get her to merge her world with mine. I need to learn to navigate her quirks. I'm not ignorant about people who need things to be organized and routine. My mother was that way. She still is. I lived with it all through my childhood.

My father is a saint who adores my mother and caters to her every whim. Drake and I were raised to be respectful of her idiosyncrasies and treat her like a queen.

Nevertheless, I know it will be hard for Faye to accept another person into her space and doubly difficult since it makes more sense for her to move into my home than for me to move into her small apartment.

It's shocking that I'm plotting so hard to reach this end goal. I've never considered moving a woman into my home. Not even Bethany. Now, I understand completely why. She wasn't right. None of them were.

Faye is right. She's mine. I'm feeling so damn posses-sive that I'm hugging her too tightly, making her whimper and squirm until I release my grip a bit.

I smile as I think about clearing out several of my drawers. They're half full anyway. I don't need all of them. And my closet. Faye can have whatever side she wants. Most of the bathroom drawers are empty. It's a huge bathroom with two sinks and a walk-in shower for two.

My bed is king-sized. Anything smaller would look silly in a room this large, but now I'm kind of wishing the bed was a twin so she can't escape my touch.

Faye can meet with Eileen to discuss any dietary issues she has and let Eileen know what foods she prefers. I wonder what she does for lunch. Does she go out with co-workers or pack something at home? Does she cook dinner for herself, or is she more of a frozen TV dinner kind of gal?

There are so many things I don't know about this amazing woman I'm holding in my arms, but none of those things matter. All that matters is that I feel a connection with her that goes deeper than I ever imag-ined possible.

She's the perfect submissive for me. As exasperating as I used to think it would be to train a submissive, I'm realizing that's not the case at all with Faye. For one thing, she easily falls into line with my demands. I didn't need to spend days or hours teaching her how to kneel. She assumed the positions I put her in instantly and held them until I gave her permission to move.

My cock is hard. I need to think about something more mundane than her submission, but that's difficult now that we're in my bed, and I'm picturing her spread eagle, her wrists and ankles secured to the four corners.

My mind wanders to visions of her sitting naked on the vanity chair in the bathroom while I brush out her hair. I switch to picturing her on her knees in the shower, looking up at me, palms open on her thighs, knees wide, lips parted, pussy dripping for attention.

I want to sit her on the vanity, spread her open, and eat her out while she holds on to the edge of the counter.

I'm insatiable. I haven't spoken to her about any of this. What if she balks? What if it's too overwhelming, and she wants to go back to her apartment, where she has a routine that calms her?

I will learn to establish a routine that makes her happy. I want to be the one who can calm and soothe her. It might take some convincing, but I'm up to the challenge.

My home is closer to the laboratory where she works. *Ha.* One point for me.

When she's not at work, she won't have to lift a finger. Eileen will take care of everything else—two points for me —unless Faye actually loves cooking or finds cleaning bathrooms cathartic. There's also the possibility that she can't stand having someone else in the house.

I need to tread carefully. Eileen's presence probably won't bother Faye because Eileen is mostly here when Faye is at work. I hate cooking, so it would never occur to me that someone else might enjoy it. If Faye loves cooking, we'll make that work. At least Eileen can do the shopping and leave everything Faye needs ready in the fridge.

I close my eyes. I need to slow my mind down and get some sleep. It's early for me. I don't usually go to bed until three in the morning. On the nights the club is open, it takes me until at least three to wind down. On the other nights of the week, I usually stay up pretty late just to keep myself on some kind of schedule.

I'm nearly as drained as Faye tonight, though. Dominating her took a lot out of me because I had to pay such close attention to every nuance to be sure I didn't push her too far.

I take deep breaths, letting them out slowly. Faye's breathing is even. She's in a deep sleep. I let myself join her.

# CHAPTER 17

## FAYE

I'm too warm. My pillow smells off. It seems softer than usual. And why does it feel like something is tangled around me? It's not my nightgown. It's heavy and tight.

Suddenly, I bolt awake, gasping for oxygen as fear consumes me. I sit upright so fast I make myself dizzy. My eyes are wide as I take in my surroundings. I have no idea where I am. Shit. Was I kidnapped? Drugged?

"Faye..." Someone touches me.

I jerk my gaze to the side, scared out of my mind.

"It's me, Faye. Easton. You're in my bed in my house."

I stare at him, trying to catch my breath as memories flood back. The roses... The club... The scene... Holy hell, I was naked in front of anyone who wanted to watch.

I grip my thighs together, arousal washing through me instantly at the memory. I don't remember anything after he released me from the ceiling.

Panic seeps in even though it's irrational. This is Easton. I'm safe. He wouldn't hurt me.

Easton sits up. He sets a hand gently on my back, drawing my attention to the fact that I'm naked. I never sleep naked.

I look around the room. The sun is up. The blinds are closed, but light is coming around them—enough for me to see clearly. I was seriously out of it when we got here. How did I end up in bed without any awareness?

He obviously undressed me. Did we...?

"Take some deep breaths, baby. I know you're confused. You were dead asleep when we got here. I carried you to bed."

"I'm naked."

"I undressed you, baby."

"Did we have sex?" I blurt out.

"God, no." He frowns. "I would never violate you when you weren't conscious, Faye. All I did was remove your street clothes, tuck you in, and snuggle against you." He pulls the covers down to his thighs. "See? I slept in my briefs."

I'm shaking as I slide back under the covers and pull them up to my chin. It's weird how I could let dozens of people see me naked and on the edge of orgasm last night, but now I'm shy in Easton's bed, where he's the only one who can see me.

He drops onto his side next to me, propping his head on his palm. He sets a hand gently on my hip. "You okay?"

"I'm not sure."

"You've been asleep nine hours. It's eight in the morning. What time do you usually get up on Sundays?"

I turn to look at him. Is he making fun of me? I don't think so. He looks serious.

He continues, "Faye, I want to adjust my schedule to help you feel comfortable. I also want to keep a close eye on you this morning. You're very suspectable to sub drop. I don't ever want you to come to the club on a weekday. You would never make it to work the next day."

I nod. He's right. I'm confused, but I don't feel as bad as I did last weekend when this happened. "I think I'm okay."

"Tell me what I can do to make you comfortable. What do you like for breakfast?"

I lick my lips. "Juice, eggs, bacon, and toast."

"Done. Tea?"

"Yes, after I eat. Do you have those things?"

"Yes, baby. I planned for anything, and I knew you liked tea. I got the same black tea I saw you drinking at your apartment and an assortment of herbal teas and green tea because you mentioned them when we were at the bakery."

I nod. "Thank you."

He's being so sweet. I'm totally out of my element, but he's trying so hard to make everything better for me. He can't begin to understand how fast my heart is racing or how hard this is for me.

I'm not in my apartment or my bed. I'm naked. I'm not used to sleeping with someone. I've never slept with someone in my life. Though apparently, I slept just fine with Easton.

I feel rested. I'm not as groggy as I was last week. "I think I'm okay," I repeat.

"Good. Do you want to take a shower? I brought your bag up from the car. Or do you like to eat first?"

I stare at him. He's really trying to be sweet. It's endearing, and it's working. He's helping me feel welcome. He needs input. He can't help me if I don't give him information. "I usually put workout clothes on, eat, and then go for a run if it's nice, or use my treadmill if it's cold or raining."

He smiles. "I can make that happen. I have a gym."

I gasp. "In your house?"

"Yes." He chuckles. "I'll give you a tour. I have a rather large home, Faye. Remember, Drake and I made it big at a young age and never stopped."

I nod. "So, do you work? I mean, like when you're not at the club...?" My face heats. That's a dumb question. I rush to cover it up. "Never mind. That's ridiculous. I'm sure the club is more than a full-time job."

He smiles and rubs my hip. "It's a reasonable question, baby. Drake and I are working on a new app. It's about half done. We work together at his house or mine during the week. We aren't in a hurry, but we're always working on something new as soon as we finish one. It sometimes takes about a year."

"Wow. You two are serious brainiacs."

He grins. "Says the woman with a PhD in biology."

"Well, my job isn't as lucrative as yours. I can tell you that."

"Your job is far more important, Faye."

I shrug.

"How about if I go downstairs and start breakfast so you can have some time to use the bathroom and put some clothes on."

I nod. "Thank you." Why do I feel so bashful and awkward?

He kisses my forehead and slides out of bed. I watch

him as he heads for the bathroom. He doesn't even shut the door all the way, so I hear the toilet flush and water run in the sink. Then he's back. He opens a drawer, pulls out clothes, and quickly puts on a T-shirt and workout shorts.

He returns to me, leans his hands on the bed, and kisses me on the lips. "Take your time, baby."

I stare at the doorway for a long time after he leaves. It's like a storm went through here. I'm unsettled and nervous. I'm also grateful. He couldn't be more accommodating and charming.

When I think I can manage, I pull the covers back and slide off the edge of the bed. I spot my bag near the foot of the bed, grab it, and hurry into the bathroom, where I close and lock the door. We're seriously going to have to talk about this sleeping naked thing. It's not going to work for me.

I feel out of sorts, even alone in the bathroom, as I rush to use the toilet before yanking open my bag and pulling out tight yoga pants, a sports bra, and a tank top. The reason I packed these things was because I envisioned myself going straight home when I woke up and figured I might as well be ready to work out when I got there. That doesn't seem to be the way Easton pictured this morning going. Luckily, I packed jeans, a shirt, and a sweater, too, just in case.

I pull on socks and tennis shoes before facing the mirror. Sheesh. My hair is wild. It takes me several minutes to run my brush through it and pull it up in a high ponytail. I wash my face, brush my teeth, and stare at myself. I have on no makeup. I don't wear makeup to work out, but I don't work out with men, either. Should I at least put on mascara?

No. That would be silly. If he wants to spend time with me, he's going to have to get used to me without makeup. I'm not particularly obsessive about it.

I find my clothes from last night, tuck everything in my bag, and zip it back up so I won't leave piles of stuff all over his room. I stare at the bed for a moment and then can't refrain from making it. I hope he doesn't think I'm overstepping.

Finally, I take a deep breath and venture out of the room. I stop dead as soon as I step into the hallway. Holy cow. This house is huge. There are so many rooms. I head in the direction of sunlight and find myself at the top of a gorgeous ornate winding staircase.

I head down it, with my hand on the banister for balance, while I swing my head all around, admiring the chandelier over the foyer, the expensive tile floor, and the double front doors.

I knew Easton and Drake had made a lot of money, but it didn't occur to me how loaded they actually are. I follow the scent of bacon until I finally step into the kitchen.

My eyes are wide. Sheesh. It's gigantic. Easton lives here alone?

He must have heard me because he spins around, spatula in hand. He grins. "Hey. I hope you don't mind your bacon crispy."

"That's how I like it." I approach him.

"And your eggs?"

"Any way is fine as long as they aren't runny."

He has a carton of eggs on the counter and a bowl next to them. He nods toward it. "Want to whisk them for me?"

"Sure." I watch him pull the bacon out of the pan and

put it on a paper towel. Grease has splattered all around the counter, but other than that, the kitchen is immaculate. "Do you normally cook?" I ask as I crack the eggs.

"No. Never." He winces. "I have a housekeeper. She does all the cooking."

I stiffen and look around.

"She's not here today. She usually works Monday through Friday and a few hours on Saturday. She leaves me meals for the rest of the weekend. I told her not to come in today because I thought it might make you uncomfortable."

I turn to him, hesitate, and then wrap my arms around his middle.

He sets the spatula down and turns fully toward me, embracing me in his huge arms. He kisses the top of my head. "I want you to feel at home."

I tip my head back and look at him. "You can't seriously mean for me to stay here more than a few hours."

He swallows hard and holds me tighter. "Baby, I want you to move in."

I gasp. "Move in? We just met." Panic seizes me.

"I'm not saying you have to do it today. I'll be patient. I'm just telling you so you'll know what my intentions are. If I had my way, we would go pack up your shit right now and move it in. But I know that's too fast for you. I won't rush you, but I won't hesitate to tell you how I feel."

"Might I point out we haven't even had sex yet?" I can't help but chuckle, though I'm shocked by my ability to do so when I should be in a full panic, running from the house.

He shrugs. "Semantics."

"You would make that kind of a commitment to a woman you haven't had sex with?"

"Yep."

"What if I suck at it? What if we're not compatible?"

"You won't suck at it, and we're already so compatible it's bonkers."

In a way, I know he's right. I've certainly never felt like this before. Still, I can't just move in. "Easton..."

He kisses my head again and turns back to the bacon. "Don't fret. We'll work it out. One day at a time. Eggs. Jogging. Those are our current goals."

"I think maybe we should add sex to that list."

He grins at me. "What time on Saturdays do you normally reserve for sex?"

I swat at him and turn to whisk the eggs before muttering, "Seven in the morning. You missed your window."

He laughs. "Dammit."

We finish cooking seamlessly together as if we do this every weekend. Thirty minutes later, we've eaten, cleaned up, and we're sitting in his amazing breakfast nook. I have my feet on the bench, my knees pulled up to my chest, and I'm sipping tea. He's drinking his second cup of coffee.

He scoots closer to me on the corner bench and strokes a lock of my hair that's dangling over my shoulder from my ponytail. "Tell me about the rest of your Saturday. What's the schedule?"

I take another sip of tea and set the mug on the table, dropping my feet to the floor. "It seems kind of silly when I think about it."

"It's not silly. It's who you are. I want to adjust myself to your schedule as much as I can. I want you to be comfortable in my home. I want you to be able to make this your home, too."

I meet his gaze. "I don't know how well I can share my life with another person, Easton, but I'll try. Just be patient with me."

"Okay, baby. Want to go work out?"

# CHAPTER 18

FAYE

I feel so much better after an hour in Easton's home gym. I've never heard of someone having all this equipment in their house. Not only did I use his treadmill, but he has a step machine and an elliptical. I used both for ten minutes each to try them out.

All the while, I had to work hard to pay attention to my footing so I didn't slide off the back of the treadmill and seriously injure myself. It was difficult with Easton pumping iron behind me. I could see him in the floor-to-ceiling mirrors. The man lifts some serious weights.

When I'm done, I'm dripping with sweat, and I guzzle a bottle of water while sitting on a weight bench, watching Easton finish. It's not a hardship. He's damn sexy, even sweaty.

He finishes and comes to me—stalks toward me, really —slowly, making me tremble. As soon as he's close enough, he snatches me off the bench, pulls me into his arms, and kisses me as though he's waited a lifetime to do so.

I'm moaning in his arms by the time he releases my lips. I struggle, trying to free myself. "I'm disgusting."

"That's not true. You're hot."

"Hot and sweaty, and I smell."

He shakes his head. "Nope. Just hot. The ponytail has made my dick hard since you first stepped into the kitchen. I thought I would drop weights on my feet, watching it sway behind you as you jogged. And do you have any idea how fucking tight and muscular your ass is? You're lucky I didn't drag you to the floor, strip you down, and fuck you right on the mat."

I suck in a breath. "Maybe you should do that."

He lifts a brow.

I shake my head as if clearing the stupidity of my request. "I need a shower."

"Mmm. I'll agree to that if you'll let me join you."

I saw his shower. It's huge. We can both definitely use it at the same time. "I'll agree to that if you're finally going to get naked in front of me. This relationship is very heavy on the naked Faye and very light on the naked Easton."

He chuckles. "I'll agree to that if you let me spread you out on the bed and eat your pussy until you scream afterward."

I shake my head. "I already made the bed."

He tips his head back and laughs hard.

I can't keep from joining him.

He kisses me. "I bet we could mess it up and make it again. Or better yet, we could mess it up so much that we need to throw the sheets in the washer and remake it with fresh sheets."

"Mmm. Let's see how the shower goes first," I tease.

He slides a hand down and pinches my ass. "Sassy girl."

I yelp and jump out of his reach before turning and running from the room. He's brought out a weird, playful side of me. Once again, I don't know who I am. I can hear him behind me, but he lets me escape. I rush to the stairs and look over my shoulder as I take them two at a time.

Easton lets me make it all the way to the bathroom before he reaches out, wraps an arm around me, and hauls me against his chest. He kisses my neck and then licks me behind the ear.

With frantic movements, he pulls my shirt over my head and then groans. "Fuck. I've wanted to see this sports bra since you first stepped into the kitchen. So sexy." He dips a finger under the bottom and teases my breasts, and then he grabs the elastic and pulls it over my head.

He rounds to my front and tugs my tight black pants down my body, taking my panties with them.

I giggle and hold his shoulders when he has to stop to remove my shoes and socks before he can finish stripping me of my pants.

I shudder when he steps back and lets his gaze roam up and down my body. "Faye..."

"Once again, I'm naked, and you're fully clothed." I manage to keep my hands at my sides. The instinct to cover myself is strong, but it's absurd at this point, and besides, he makes me feel like a goddess when he looks at me with those smoldering eyes.

Without taking his gaze off me, he kicks off his shoes and begins stripping. He leaves his shorts for last and reaches into the shower to turn it on before facing me again.

"Take them off," I say in a wobbly voice I don't recognize.

He steps closer. "You do it."

I shudder, but I'm salivating at the same time. I grab the elastic of his shorts and ease them down his hips, taking his underwear with them. When I get the fabric stuck against his enormous erection, I pull his shorts back up a few inches and lift them over the tip of his penis before continuing to lower them.

I hold my breath, trying not to react. Until last weekend, I had never seen a penis before. I saw several that night, but none compare to Easton's. Sheesh. It's huge.

Easton takes my hand in his, eases it to his erection, and wraps my fingers around the base. He folds his hand over mine and guides me to stroke up and down his shaft.

A soft moan escapes his lips, making my pussy clench.

Easton growls before easing my hand off the tip. "Shower, baby, now."

We step around the corner into the dual heads of spray. It feels so good hitting my shoulders, but I'm so hot we probably should have taken a cold shower.

Easton's gaze is intense as he silently pulls the ponytail holder out of my hair and sets it on the ledge. He pours shampoo into his palm. "Turn around, baby."

I face the wall, moaning when he massages the shampoo into my scalp. "Sorry, you're going to smell like me today. We'll order the products you prefer so they will be here tomorrow."

Tomorrow... Will I seriously still be here tomorrow? It's mind-boggling.

By the time he finishes shampooing my hair and

putting in conditioner, I'm boneless. I have to grab the soap ledge to brace myself when he starts soaping my body.

My heart is racing. I'm so aroused. I've never wanted anything more in my life. I want him inside me.

When he's done, I spin around and grab the shampoo. I point at the ledge. "Sit."

He chuckles as he obeys me.

"I can't possibly reach your hair if you're not sitting," I inform him.

He grabs my hips and leans his head forward so I can shampoo his hair. I apply conditioner next and then pick up the liquid soap as he stands. He takes it from me. "I'll finish. If you touch me any more than you already have, I'll come before we make it to the sheets."

I purse my lips and back into the spray of water to rinse my hair, watching him. His body is an art form. His shaft is long and wide. Hard as a rock. I want it in me. I'm not scared.

Okay, maybe a little.

Easton hurries to finish, turns off the water, and grabs a towel. When I reach to take it from him, he swats my hand out of the way and dries me himself.

"So controlling," I tease.

He gives me a hungry gaze, making me shut up. "Baby, you have not seen controlling yet. Are you sure you're ready to take me into your body?"

"Yes, Sir."

He flinches at the use of that term of respect. A low growl escapes his lips again as he quickly dries himself with the same towel. He drops the towel on the floor, takes my hand, and drags me into the bedroom.

I nearly laugh as he tugs the bedding off so hard it all

falls on the floor, leaving nothing but the fitted sheet. "Hey, I worked hard on that," I joke.

He grabs me by the hips, spins me around, and deposits me in the middle of the bed. He crawls over me, straddling me with his hands and knees, and stares down at me. "I'm never going to get enough of you, Faye."

"You haven't even had me yet. Maybe it won't be that great." I'm mostly serious. This is a concern of mine.

He shakes his head. "In a few minutes, you will never have that thought again." His lips crush mine, the kiss filled with desperation. By the time he's done, I'm limp and needy even though he hasn't touched any other part of me.

He climbs off the bed, yanks open the drawer of his nightstand, and pulls out a condom. His intense gaze is on me as he tears it open with his teeth, pulls it out, and rolls it down his shaft. He takes his time, giving me a show. A very sexy show.

"Spread your legs, baby," he orders. "Wide. I want to see how wet you are."

I part my thighs, bend my knees, and open myself up for him.

"Good girl. Arms above your head. You may not touch me this first time. If your pretty fingers even skim my shoulders, I'll come."

I lift my arms, trembling with need. His orders make me so damn hot for him.

He kneels between my legs and leans over to suck one of my nipples into his mouth, making me arch and cry out. He releases it with a pop. "God, I love how noisy you are. I want you to scream. No one can hear you. Don't hold back, Faye."

I'm not sure I'm capable of being aware of my noises. I certainly can't hold them back.

He sucks my other nipple until I'm writhing and desperate. Finally, he releases it and moves down my body. He flattens himself between my legs, palms my thighs, and holds me down a second before his mouth crashes onto my pussy.

I arch nearly off the bed. The only reason I'm still touching the mattress is because he's holding me down. It's hard to keep my hands above my head, but I grab a pillow behind me and fist it to help remind myself not to lower my arms.

Easton thrusts his tongue into me before returning to torment my clit, flicking it and circling it with his tongue.

I moan low and deep when he pushes a finger into me.

He lets go of my clit and looks up at me. "Jesus, you're so tight, Faye."

What did he expect?

He adds a second finger, making me moan louder. I had no idea it would feel this good. I've used my vibrator inside me, but it's not nearly as wide as his shaft. I can't think. It feels so good. "I'm going to come," I tell him.

"Do it, baby. Come for me. It will make your body relax a bit before I enter you."

I hold my breath when he curls his fingers and drags them along the top of my channel. That's all it takes to push me over the edge. My vision blurs as my orgasm consumes me.

He doesn't stop. His fingers work me harder, thrusting in and out of me. At some point, he adds a third, and I clench down on them, close to another orgasm.

Easton abruptly pulls them out and climbs up my body. He hovers over me, holding my gaze.

I'm panting. "Please," I beg.

"Are you sure?"

"Yes. God, yes." I defy his order and bring my hands to his neck, trying to lure him down. "I want this, Easton. I want it more than anything in my life."

"I'll never be able to let you go, Faye."

I stare into his eyes. He's serious, but I can't fathom a world in which he lets me go right now anyway. "Make love to me."

He drops his hips, lines his erection up with my channel, and rubs the tip along my folds.

I moan. It feels so good, but it's not enough. I thrust my hips upward, trying to get more friction or perhaps cause him to slip inside.

I'm gripping his neck as though it's a lifeline, but he doesn't seem to mind. I lift my hips again. "Easton, I need you."

He thrusts into me. Hard and fast. It takes my breath away. It's so incredibly tight. My channel is pulsing around him, adjusting to his girth. It doesn't hurt. It's just tight.

"Faye..." He cups my face. "Baby..."

"I'm okay. Better than okay. Do it again."

He eases out and thrusts back deeper this time.

I moan, my eyes rolling back. I had no idea it would feel this good. Shouldn't it hurt? It doesn't. Maybe there was a twinge for a second, but it's gone. Now, it's all bliss.

I can't control the sounds coming out of my mouth as he thrusts in and out of me. It's heavenly. Why did I wait thirty-one years to experience this? Then again, it probably wouldn't have been this good with another man.

Easton stops moving, holding himself deep inside me. He's panting and staring down at me.

I whimper and squirm.

"Hold on a second, baby." The look on his face makes my chest tighten. He's undone. He's trying not to come. I love that I affect him so much.

Suddenly, he grabs my hips, and before I know it, he has flipped us. I'm on top of him. Straddling him. His erection never slipped out of me. My hair is hanging down around me. It's wild and damp and untamed.

Easton gathers most of it in his hands and holds it to one side as he grips my shoulders. "Ride me, Faye. Do what feels good. Grind your pussy down until you come."

I'm too stunned to move. He wants me to ride him? I mean, I understand the concept, but I never pictured myself on top like this.

He smiles. "You can do it, baby. I promise you will love it. When you're on top, you control the pace, the depth, and the rhythm."

Mmm. I pull my feet up and plant them alongside his hips before lifting up a few inches. When I lower back down, I nearly giggle. I feel powerful. He's letting me control this.

"That's it, baby. Do it again."

I lift up again until he's almost entirely out of me, leaving just the tip inside. I stare down at his shaft, which is hovering at my entrance. It looks far too large to fit inside me, and yet it does. I slam back down.

*Oh. My. God.* It feels so good. I tip my head back and arch my chest forward so I can grind my clit against the base of his shaft. *Amazing.*

He holds my hair with one hand and brings the other

around to cup my breast, flicking my nipple, doubling my arousal.

"Easton..."

"God, you're gorgeous, Faye. I'm never going to let you go. You're mine. I'm going to take control now, baby. I'm going to fuck you until you scream."

I don't know what he means, but he releases my breast and my hair, grabs my hips, holds me steady, and lifts his torso up and down, fucking me from beneath just like he promised.

I hold his gaze for as long as I can until my channel grips him harder as if it's not in my control. My orgasm is right there, and then it peaks. He senses this moment, thrusts harder, and then holds me down so his shaft is fully embedded in me.

I scream as I come, my channel pulsing around his erection. It's so much more intense than the orgasms I've had without him filling me. Seconds after the pulsing begins, Easton comes, too. He cries out, a primal sound that fills the room and probably the house.

I'm shaking violently with chills as the waves subside. Easton lifts me off his shaft and lowers me to my side next to him. He reaches over the end of the bed to snag the edge of a blanket and pulls it over us before hauling me into his arms, chest to chest, and holding me tightly.

He kisses my temple. "Faye..." The one word is so reverent.

It takes me a long time to stop shaking. Eventually, I relax into his embrace. I'm aware his erection is against my thigh, still hard. "Didn't you come?" I ask softly.

He chuckles. "I came, baby. My cock is just still hard. It's probably going to stay hard for a month."

I snuggle deeper against him. I feel oddly peaceful. Human. I just did a normal human thing. Maybe I can do more normal human things.

# CHAPTER 19

## FAYE

"Are you sure about this?" I'm standing in my bedroom Sunday afternoon, spinning around. I can't seem to make decisions. I'm biting my thumbnail.

Easton has two large suitcases open on my bed and four boxes taped and ready on the floor. He comes to me, grips my shoulders, and meets my gaze. "We aren't breaking your lease, baby. You're just bringing some things to my house. Don't panic. Nothing is permanent until you decide you want it to be."

I draw in a deep breath. He's right, but I'm so out of my element. I've slept in his bed for two nights. Last night, I went to the club with him, but I spent the entire time in his apartment, mostly reading.

I learned he has room service provided by the first-floor restaurant, so I ordered dinner, dessert, and snacks. He checked on me a dozen times but didn't want me to play because I'm so deeply affected when I do a scene that I was still hovering in subspace from the night before.

After two full days with him, I've agreed to move some things to his house and stay there. This is huge. I haven't told a single soul about any of this, not even Trinity. I'm not ready to tell anyone yet. It's private.

I'm not the sort of person who owns a ton of clothes. I have what I need, and that's about it, so it's easy for Easton to pack for me while I stand in the middle of the room and fret.

I watch as he grabs handfuls of clothes out of my closet, hangers and all, and lowers them into a suitcase. Suddenly, he stops moving and stares at the pile. Slowly, he picks up the top item. The blue jacket. He takes it off the hanger and holds it up. "You kept it..." he murmurs before turning to me.

I frown. "How do you know about that jacket?"

He drops it onto the pile and comes to me. He cups my face. "You don't know."

"What don't I know?"

"I'm the one who left that for you on your locker the day those idiots intentionally ran into you in the cafeteria and caused your tray to fly up so that spaghetti spilled down your white blouse. I watched in horror. I wanted to kill them, but I was too fucking weak and stupid back then. Hell, the same idiots bullied me. I nearly died as you ran from the cafeteria. I knew you were mortified, and your shirt was ruined, so I hung my jacket on the handle of your locker while you were in the bathroom."

I can't breathe. I'm so shocked. "It was you..."

"You kept the jacket..." He pulls me into his arms and holds me tight.

"It meant the world to me," I tell his chest. "I still pull it out and wear it when I need comforting."

He rocks me back and forth for a long time. Somehow, we've added this odd new connection. He's so damn kind that he even saved me from embarrassment sixteen years ago, and I never knew it.

Finally, he tips me back, kisses me gently, and turns silently back to the suitcases.

When he's done, he closes everything up and makes a few trips to his SUV while I walk through my apartment. I'm not making any life-altering decisions here. I can always move back in if it doesn't work out, but something has changed between us. I feel different. I'm not as scared.

I'm quiet on the way back to Easton's house. It's more of a mansion. There are so many rooms. He says I can turn one of them into an office or whatever kind of space I want so that I have a room totally my own where I can go and regroup at any time.

He's so thoughtful. During the drive, he holds my hand a lot, not interrupting my thoughts.

By dinner time, my clothes are all put away in the drawers he emptied for me and inside his closet. The jacket is hanging right in the center between my clothes and his. My toiletries have a place in his bathroom. The nightstand on one side of the bed has my books and phone charger.

We order Chinese and sit in the breakfast nook, sharing various containers. We watch a movie like regular people—though most regular people don't have an amazing theater room like Easton has.

It's nice sitting curled up next to him on his black leather couch in the totally dark room. Throughout the romcom, he strokes my arm and repeatedly kisses the top of my head as if he can't get enough of me.

"What time do you like to be in bed on work nights?" he asks when the movie ends.

"Ten. I need eight hours. I'm useless without enough sleep."

"Then let's get you ready for bed." He stands, helps me up, and takes my hand.

"It's only nine," I tell him after I brush my teeth and glance at the clock.

"Yep." He wiggles his brows at me, and my pussy reacts.

I giggle. "So, you're saying you intend to have your way with me, and it's going to take an hour?" I tease.

He drags me into the bedroom and pulls my shirt over my head.

I try not to wince when he tosses it on the floor. I can be messy. Sure, I can.

He pops my bra off next and flings it toward my shirt. "Don't worry. I'll pick it up after you fall asleep."

I shrug as though it makes no difference to me.

He chuckles. "And to answer your other question, it will only take me about two minutes to come, but it's going to take you thirty, and I'm leaving fifteen minutes for you to catch your breath and get to sleep afterward. You'll be asleep by ten."

"Thirty?" I giggle. "I'm about to come now just from the mention of sex."

"Mmm..." He removes the rest of my clothes. I've realized he likes to undress me. He likes to dress me, too. And he always has me completely naked before he strips.

"Climb up on the bed. Lie in the middle, arms and legs spread wide."

I bite my lip as I obey him. So, this is going to be kinky...

He pulls something out from under the bed. I can't see it, but a moment later, he's holding up four cuffs.

As I glance at the four posts, goosebumps rise all over my body. It's no wonder he has a four-poster bed.

"I'm going to restrain you and tease you until you beg me to let you come," he informs me as he grabs my wrist and gets to work.

By the time I'm completely secured, spread wide open, I'm so horny I could come with just a touch.

I'm glad when Easton strips, also. I like to look at his body. He's like a god, all muscles and tightness. He rolls on a condom before he climbs up to kneel between my legs.

I arch my chest up and moan. "Easton..."

"You're so responsive. I haven't even touched you yet, and you're already about to come."

He's right. I should be embarrassed, but I'm not nearly as flustered by my body's reactions to him anymore.

I learn something in the next forty-five minutes. Easton can be very precise. The man teases my body until I'm writhing so much he has to admonish me so I don't tug too hard and hurt myself. He's got an uncanny ability to touch me softly in one small spot. A nipple, my lips, a flick over my clit. Over and over until I'm begging.

When he finally thrusts into me, I'm so horny that I come instantly. All I can see is bright lights flickering around me as my eyes roll back.

He's so aroused from tormenting me that he comes minutes later, and he has us both cleaned up and snuggled under the covers at a quarter to ten.

I start giggling uncontrollably. "Are you always that precise, or did you do all that just for me?"

"I can be precise if I need to, baby." He kisses me. "See? You'll be asleep by ten and bright-eyed at six. You can get your workout in, eat breakfast, and be at work right on time."

I'm grinning as I relax against him. "I'm not going to get used to sleeping naked," I say, wrinkling my nose.

"You will." He runs his hand down to my bottom and squeezes it. "I like you naked."

I sigh. Maybe he's right. After all, I've slept naked several times now, and it didn't disturb me a bit. His sheets are expensive and divine. They feel good against my bare skin. "Are you ever going to give me my vibrator back?"

"Nope. You're still not permitted to come without me. Your orgasms are mine. Maybe I'll let you use it while I watch one of these days, but you can't have it to use without me, naughty girl."

I bite my lip to keep from chuckling as I snuggle into him.

Within minutes, my eyes are heavy, and somehow, my brain stops running. I fall asleep right on time.

# CHAPTER 20

*TWO WEEKS LATER...*

Faye

"Yep. That sounds great. Thank you so much, Eileen." I'm sitting in the breakfast nook—my favorite spot in the house—one leg swinging, one knee pulled up to my chest. I have the most delicious mug of herbal tea steaming in front of me, the scent filling the room, and my favorite science magazine is open on the table.

It's Saturday morning. I quietly slid out of bed at seven and started my routine. Easton is still sleeping. He didn't get home until after three. But I've gotten comfortable with roaming his house alone, especially on the weekends when he needs to sleep and I don't have work.

It's still weird. I don't think of this house as mine. I feel like I'm kind of just staying here for a while. I'm happy, but I'm not ready to give up my apartment.

Easton bends over backward to ensure my needs are met. He's very polite and attentive to my weird desire to maintain structure. This is why I've already eaten, worked out, and showered.

I adore Eileen. She's the best and has confided in me how relieved she is that Easton has finally met a woman who makes him happy. Apparently, he was in a sour mood for a long time while he was dating Bethany.

Eileen makes my life easier. I'm not a great cook, so I usually stuck to the basics and ate a lot of frozen foods. She's the most amazing cook. She makes our evenings so smooth since she always has dinner ready. She has even shifted her hours so that she has breakfast for me and my lunch ready.

We argued about that part one evening for quite some time. I felt weird, causing her to change for me. I can handle breakfasts, but she insisted it was no problem, and she wanted to do whatever it took to be helpful.

I don't look at the clock as often. It doesn't matter that I don't sit down with my tea and magazine at some precise hour. In fact, I have more free time than I did in my apartment since Eileen does all the laundry and cleaning.

Sometimes, I feel weird about being waited on, but Eileen takes all the weirdness away with a wave of the hand. *"It's my job. It's what I love."*

Eileen chuckles.

I look up from my tea.

"You didn't hear a word I said, did you?" she asks.

I flush. "Oh, uh. Sorry. I was in my head."

She's still chuckling and steps closer, hands on her hips. "Before you went into your head, dear, I was asking you about the menu for the coming week, and you agreed without hearing it."

I smile and shrug. "That's because all your cooking is amazing, and I don't care what you make. I'm just so grateful someone else is doing it. You have no idea. I feel like I woke up one morning, and suddenly, I'm a princess. You're spoiling me."

She smiles warmly. "You deserve to be spoiled, Faye. Have I mentioned how glad I am that Easton met you? He deserves to be spoiled, too."

The doorbell rings, and we both glance in that direction, which I've always thought was hilarious since looking at the other side of the kitchen doesn't reveal a single piece of information about who's at the door.

I climb out of my corner of the nook. "I'll see who it is."

"Are you sure? I can get it."

Eileen is in the middle of making bread. The dough is on the island. I shake my head. "I've got it."

I hurry through the house to the front door and open it without a thought.

A woman I've never seen is standing there. She looks like she's come for a high-powered job interview. She's wearing a formfitting navy dress that accentuates every perfect curve. Her nearly black hair is long and styled as though she just left a salon. Her makeup is expertly applied. She even has on heels. I wonder if she's a realtor and has come to the wrong house.

When I first opened the door, I caught a glimpse of a broad smile, but it fell instantly, and now she's frowning. "Who are you? Did Easton hire a new housekeeper?" She looks up and down my frame as though I'm nothing but trash.

Granted, I'm wearing comfortable leggings and a huge sweater. My feet are bare. My hair is up in a messy bun. I have on no makeup. But she has no right to look at me like that, nor should she be asking who I am. Who the heck is *she*?

"I'm sorry. You are...?"

She surprises me when she pushes the door open wider and steps into the house. She looks around. "Where's Easton? Is he still sleeping?" She heads for the stairs.

I'm so shocked all I can do is stand in the open doorway and watch her climb the stairs. I finally find my voice when she's about halfway up. "Uh, what are you doing?"

She turns to wink at me. "Don't you worry. I'm his girlfriend. Maybe stick to cleaning downstairs this morning."

All the air leaves my lungs. I'm so incredibly stunned I can't move. His girlfriend? Is this Bethany? She is not what I ever pictured. She's...like a wealthy model.

I'm nothing like her. Why is he even with me if he usually dates women who look like that? Insecurities flood me. I can't compete with that. If Easton likes his women all fixed up with fancy hair, nails, makeup, and designer clothes, he has chosen poorly with me.

Easton has never said a word about my style or my clothes, though one time, he told me he didn't care if I wore makeup or not, so I never do when we're at home, even though I know I look washed out without at least mascara. My eyebrows and eyelashes are blond.

The only discussion we've ever had about clothes was concerning him buying me fetish wear, which I proudly don when we go to Edge.

Eileen steps into the foyer, wiping her hands on a

towel. "Faye? Who was at the door? Why are you still standing there?"

I glance at her and then back at the steps just in time to hear Easton shout. "What the fuck, Bethany?"

I wince.

Eileen's eyes go wide. "That bitch." I've never heard Eileen cuss, but she turns to the stairs and takes them two at a time.

I finally manage to shut the door, but there's no way I'm going upstairs to join the show. I want no part in this. I know I'm not in my right mind when I start doubting Easton, but I can't help it.

He was with Bethany for six months. I've known him for three weeks. I rub my hands together and look around. I want to hide. I kind of want to leave the house, but I don't have on shoes or socks, which are both upstairs. It's too cold outside for me to leave in bare feet. I'd freeze just getting to the car.

I hear Bethany's voice. "Eileen? You're here, too? How many cleaning ladies do you need, Easton?"

I flinch. Fuck her. What a pretentious bitch. There. I've used two cuss words. In fact, I repeat them out loud. "Fuck her. What a pretentious bitch." I feel oddly better having spoken my feelings.

Bethany represents every person I've ever encountered who bullied me. She's the kind of woman who looks down on people, smirks in their face, and talks about them behind their back. She's the kind of woman who would dump spaghetti down my blouse even at this age. She's a bitch.

I'm shaking. Easton dated this woman for months. What does that say about the kind of women he dates? Not people like me. I'm the polar opposite.

Easton is shouting now, but I'm not listening to his words. I can't. I'm too upset. I don't want to be standing here when they come back down, so I rush out of the foyer, down the hallway, and into Easton's office. It's more like a library, considering how many books he has in it. It has become my second favorite room in the house because it's so warm and inviting. Dark tones. Paneling, dark hardwood floors, jewel-toned area rugs, and mahogany leather furniture.

I grab a throw blanket off the back of the couch and curl up in the corner of the leather sofa, wrapping myself in a cocoon. I'm shaking. The shouting continues, but I can't make out the words anymore. I stare out the window at the backyard.

It's so beautiful, even when nothing is in bloom. This home is peaceful and comfortable. It's clean and orderly—which I love—but it's inviting and warm at the same time. I'm happy here.

I try to tell myself Easton is with *me* now. He's not with her. But it kind of freaks me out that he was ever with her. How was he dating such a bitch for six months?

He hasn't known me very long. If that's what I'm competing against, I'll never be able to hold his attention and keep him happy. I'm never going to be sophisticated like her. I'm ordinary and boring. My idiosyncrasies will drive him crazy soon.

I flinch when I hear stomping on the stairs. I cover my ears with both hands to block out whatever might be said next. I squeeze my eyes closed and rock back and forth in the corner. My comfort level is at its lowest.

I'm not sure how much time goes by before a hand lands on my shoulder. I jerk my eyes open and drop my hands, heart racing, as I realize it's Easton. He sits next to me, his hand still on my shoulder. He's wearing sweat-pants and a T-shirt. His hair is a mess from sleeping.

His brow is furrowed. "I'm so sorry, Faye."

I stare at him and then look down. My heart is still racing.

"Baby, look at me."

I shake my head and swallow. "I can't compete with that, Easton."

"Compete with what?"

I shrug. "The makeup, hair, nails, and designer clothes. It's not me. Why are you dating me?"

His breath hitches. "Faye, I don't give a fuck about hair, makeup, and clothes. Surely you know that. I'm glad that's not you. You're a breath of fresh air. You're real. You're just you. Nothing about you is fake. Most of the reason I've fallen in love with you is because you're exactly who you present. And I'm not *dating* you."

I gasp and look at him. I'm so confused. My brain is spinning from his last two incongruent sentences. He's not dating me? And he's in love with me?

He lifts my chin. "Baby, you're my girlfriend, my lover. You live in my house. You're mine forever. You're not a passing fling. I love you—so much it scares me. I've never loved another woman. I certainly didn't love Bethany. I didn't realize how incompatible she and I were. I was just going through the motions. Bethany, I was dating. You are so much more than that."

I can't breathe.

He releases my chin, tucks his hands under me, and lifts me onto his lap. He holds me close. "I love you, Faye," he repeats. "Do you get that? You're perfect for me."

"What was she doing here?" I need to know, even though I'd rather not.

"She had it in her head that she could change and be what she thinks I wanted. She can't change, and she was never something I wanted. I want what you and I have. Basically, she missed my money."

I frown. "Your money?"

He chuckles. "Faye, if you haven't noticed, I have a lot of it."

I think about that. Duh. Of course. I'm a dolt.

"See? You don't even give a fuck about money."

"I don't need money. I have my own." I sit straighter in his lap. "I make good money at my job. I save half of it every paycheck." I'm proud of what I've become.

He smiles and kisses me gently. "I love you." He kisses me again. "I love you." And again. "I love you."

I wrap my arms around his neck and look him in the eye. He's serious. He's not playing. I'm the luckiest woman alive. "I love you, too, Easton."

His grin widens, and he blows out a relieved sigh. "You scared me there."

I giggle. "Not as much as you scared me when that crazy woman came barreling into the house and straight up the stairs as if she belonged here, and I don't."

"Well, she doesn't belong here. You do. She never belonged. You're mine. I don't know what the hell I was thinking before I met you, but I'm a better man now because of you."

I push the blanket off me, glancing behind me and trying not to wince when it lands on the floor. *Let it go.* Shaking off my need to pick it up, I turn in his lap and straddle him, rocking forward so that my pussy rubs against his cock.

He slides his hands up my back. "Naughty girl."

"Mmm." I do it again. "*Your* naughty girl."

"Damn right." His hands come to my shoulders, and he holds me down. "I think you need to be reminded why we are so good together." He slides his hands down and pushes my shirt over my head, intentionally tossing it on the floor.

I'm not wearing a bra, and I gasp as I glance at the door. "Easton..."

"Eileen left. I deadbolted the doors. No one will see us."

I glance toward the floor-to-ceiling windows. "What if the gardener comes?"

"The gardener isn't coming today, baby, and who cares? The thought of being caught naked makes you horny every time. My little exhibitionist likes the thought of possibly being exposed."

I shudder. He's right. My nipples are hard, and I rock against his cock again. "Maybe you should fuck me against the window." Who am I?

He chuckles. "Maybe I will. When did you start cussing like a sailor?"

"You should've heard me in the foyer after Bethany took off up the stairs, followed by Eileen."

"I'm sorry I missed that." He grins as he grips my ass and stands to carry me across the room. "I think I *will* fuck you against the window. I also think you should switch gears and submit to me, naughty girl."

A switch flips in my head at his command. "Yes, Sir."

"That's better." He holds me with one hand under my ass and drags one of the armchairs over to the window. Before I can process his intent, he strips me naked, leans me over the back of the chair, and restrains my ankles spread open to the legs of the chair. My ass is facing the window.

Easton pets me. "So gorgeous. So perfect. All mine."

"Yes, Sir."

"Never doubt me, baby. My heart is yours."

"Yes, Sir."

"Now, how long do you think I should tease you into submission before I fuck you clear into tomorrow?" His hand comes between my legs.

I cry out when he strokes my folds, barely grazing over my clit. "Five minutes, Sir?"

He laughs. "Try again, baby. Try again."

# AUTHOR'S NOTE

Thank you for reading Salacious Exposure. I hope you've enjoyed diving into our Seattle Doms series. Ready for more?!

## Seattle Doms:

Salacious Exposure by Becca Jameson
Salacious Desires By Kate Oliver
Salacious Attraction by Becca Jameson
Salacious Indulgence by Kate Oliver
Salacious Devotion by Becca Jameson
Salacious Surrender by Kate Oliver

**Seattle Doms:**

Salacious Exposure by Becca Jameson

Salacious Desires By Kate Oliver

Salacious Attraction by Becca Jameson

Salacious Indulgence by Kate Oliver

Salacious Devotion by Becca Jameson

Salacious Surrender by Kate Oliver

**Danger Bluff:**

Rocco

Hawking

Kestrel

Magnus

Phoenix

Caesar

**Roses and Thorns:**

Marigold

Oleander

Jasmine

Tulip

Daffodil

Lily

Roses and Thorns Box Set One

Roses and Thorns Box Set Two

**Shadowridge Guardians:**

Steele by Pepper North

Kade by Kate Oliver

Atlas by Becca Jameson

Doc by Kate Oliver

Gabriel by Becca Jameson

Talon by Pepper North

Bear by Becca Jameson

Faust by Pepper North

Storm by Kate Oliver

Blade by Pepper North

King by Kate Oliver

Rock by Becca Jameson

**Blossom Ridge:**

Starting Over

Finding Peace

Building Trust

Feeling Brave

Embracing Joy

Accepting Love

Blossom Ridge Box Set One

Blossom Ridge Box Set Two

**The Wanderers:**

Sanctuary

Surrender Box Set Four

## Open Skies:

Layover

Redeye

Nonstop

Standby

Takeoff

Jetway

Open Skies Box Set One

Open Skies Box Set Two

## Shadow SEALs:

Shadow in the Desert

Shadow in the Darkness

## Holt Agency:

Rescued by Becca Jameson

Unchained by KaLyn Cooper

Protected by Becca Jameson

Liberated by KaLyn Cooper

Defended by Becca Jameson

Unrestrained by KaLyn Cooper

## Delta Team Three (Special Forces: Operation Alpha):

Destiny's Delta

## Canyon Springs:

Caleb's Mate

Hunter's Mate

**Corked and Tapped:**

Volume One: Friday Night

Volume Two: Company Party

Volume Three: The Holidays

The Complete Set

**Project DEEP:**

Reviving Emily

Reviving Trish

Reviving Dade

Reviving Zeke

Reviving Graham

Reviving Bianca

Reviving Olivia

Project DEEP Box Set One

Project DEEP Box Set Two

**SEALs in Paradise:**

Hot SEAL, Red Wine

Hot SEAL, Australian Nights

Hot SEAL, Cold Feet

Hot SEAL, April's Fool

Hot SEAL, Brown-Eyed Girl

**Dark Falls:**

Dark Nightmares

**Club Zodiac:**

Training Sasha

Obeying Rowen

Collaring Brooke

Mastering Rayne

Trusting Aaron

Claiming London

Sharing Charlotte

Taming Rex

Tempting Elizabeth

Club Zodiac Box Set One

Club Zodiac Box Set Two

Club Zodiac Box Set Three

**The Art of Kink:**

Pose

Paint

Sculpt

**Arcadian Bears:**

Grizzly Mountain

Grizzly Beginning

Grizzly Secret

Grizzly Promise

Grizzly Survival

Grizzly Perfection

Arcadian Bears Box Set One

Arcadian Bears Box Set Two

## Sleeper SEALs:

Saving Zola

## Spring Training:

Catching Zia

Catching Lily

Catching Ava

Spring Training Box Set

## The Underground series:

Force

Clinch

Guard

Submit

Thrust

Torque

The Underground Box Set One

The Underground Box Set Two

## Wolf Masters series:

Kara's Wolves

Lindsey's Wolves

Jessica's Wolves

Alyssa's Wolves

Tessa's Wolf

Rebecca's Wolves

Melinda's Wolves

Laurie's Wolves

Amanda's Wolves

Sharon's Wolves

Wolf Masters Box Set One

Wolf Masters Box Set Two

## Claiming Her series:

The Rules

The Game

The Prize

Claiming Her Box Set

## Emergence series:

Bound to be Taken

Bound to be Tamed

Bound to be Tested

Bound to be Tempted

Emergence Box Set

## The Fight Club series:

Come

Perv

Need

Hers

Want

Lust

The Fight Club Box Set One

The Fight Club Box Set Two

**Wolf Gatherings series:**

Tarnished

Dominated

Completed

Redeemed

Abandoned

Betrayed

Wolf Gatherings Box Set One

Wolf Gathering Box Set Two

**Durham Wolves series:**

Rescue in the Smokies

Fire in the Smokies

Freedom in the Smokies

Durham Wolves Box Set

**Stand Alone Books:**

Blind with Love

Guarding the Truth

Out of the Smoke

Abducting His Mate

Wolf Trinity

Frostbitten

A Princess for Cale/A Princess for Cain

Severed Dreams

Where Alphas Dominate

# ABOUT THE AUTHOR

Becca Jameson is a USA Today best-selling author of over 150 books. She is well-known for her Wolf Masters series, her Fight Club series, and her Surrender series. She currently lives in Houston, Texas, with her husband. Two grown kids pop in every once in a while, too! She is loving this journey and has dabbled in a variety of genres, including paranormal, sports romance, military, reverse harem, dark romance, suspense, dystopian, BDSM, and Daddy Dom.

A total night owl, Becca writes late at night, sequestering herself in her office with a glass of red wine and a bar of dark chocolate, her fingers flying across the keyboard as her characters weave their own stories.

During the day--which never starts before ten in the morning!--she can be found walking, running errands, or reading in her favorite hammock chair!

*...where Alphas dominate...*

Becca's Newsletter Sign-up

Join my Facebook fan group, Becca's Bibliomaniacs, for the most up-to-date information, random excerpts while I work, giveaways, and fun release parties!

*Facebook Fan Group:*
Becca's Bibliomaniacs

*Contact Becca:*
www.beccajameson.com
beccajameson4@aol.com

f facebook.com/becca.jameson.18

X x.com/beccajameson

○ instagram.com/becca.jameson

BB bookbub.com/authors/becca-jameson

g goodreads.com/beccajameson

a amazon.com/author/beccajameson

Made in the USA
Columbia, SC
10 July 2024